Her heart stopped. *Will Austin make it back up to me? Am I stranded?*

Blood pounded in her temples. Dulcie tried her cell phone. Nothing. The fact that she was all alone in this blizzard filled her with dread. Suddenly, the sound of a car engine made her pause.

A black SUV she didn't recognize pulled to a stop in front of the house. Two men in dark clothing stepped out.

Panic surged through her and she ran back downstairs. There was no knock on the door or calling out. Instead, gunfire exploded and hit the door. The solid wood splintered, sending pieces across the room. Dulcie screamed and dove for the couch.

They had to be members of the gang and they were here to get her. They concentrated their shots around the dead bolt. They were shooting out the lock! Any minute they'd be inside. She looked around, desperately searching for somewhere to hide. There was no place. No nook or cranny. Just Austin's wide open home, the place she'd loved from the minute she saw it. Now it would be her trap.

Tanya Stowe is a Christian fiction author with an unexpected edge. She is married to the love of her life, her high school sweetheart. They have four children and twenty-one grandchildren, a true adventure. She fills her books with the unusual—mysteries and exotic travel, even a murder or two. No matter where Tanya takes you—on a trip to foreign lands or a suspenseful journey packed with danger—be prepared for the extraordinary.

Books by Tanya Stowe

Love Inspired Suspense

Mojave Rescue
Fatal Memories
Killer Harvest
Vanished in the Mountains

VANISHED IN THE MOUNTAINS

TANYA STOWE

LOVE INSPIRED SUSPENSE

INSPIRATIONAL ROMANCE

LOVE INSPIRED® SUSPENSE
INSPIRATIONAL ROMANCE

PLEASE RECYCLE

THIS PRODUCT IS RECYCLABLE

Recycling programs for this product may not exist in your area.

ISBN-13: 978-1-335-40505-0

Vanished in the Mountains

Copyright © 2021 by Tanya Stowe

This edition published by arrangement with Harlequin Books S.A.

For questions and comments about the quality of this book, please contact us at CustomerService@Harlequin.com.

Love Inspired
22 Adelaide St. West, 40th Floor
Toronto, Ontario M5H 4E3, Canada
www.Harlequin.com

Printed in U.S.A.

And that he might make known the riches of his glory on the vessels of mercy, which he had afore prepared unto glory.

–Romans 9:23

For my husband, Gary,
and one of the trips of our lifetime.

ONE

Dulcie Parker wound her long curls into a tight bun on top of her head and gave it one last pat. Messy, soft buns were the "in" look right now but for her, the tighter the better. First off, her super-curly hair was messy enough and second, she'd found that the sterner, harsher look worked best for her job. In fact, she considered it part of her work uniform: a tight bun, black pants, a crisp white button-front shirt and a black jacket. As a fairly young domestic violence counselor, she needed to be taken seriously, not only by the men she often met but also by her coworkers who considered her too young and inexperienced.

As if anyone is too young to know that words and fists hurt. Her cultured university-professor father taught her that lesson.

She closed her eyes and forced those thoughts from her mind. Going down that path was not the way to start out her workday…one that would end up with her being late to the shelter if she didn't get a move on. With one last push to a misbehaving curl, she flipped off the bathroom light.

As she entered the small living room of her apartment, she frowned. An envelope lay on the floor by the door.

Puzzled, she picked up the plain white envelope, ripped open the seal and removed a single piece of paper folded neatly into thirds. A message was printed vertically down the middle of the sheet.

Mind your own business or you'll become a Missing One.

Dulcie's fingers trembled as she read the words.

*A missing one...*the exact words her client Doris Begay had used.

In Dulcie's line of work, threats came with the job. She'd been yelled at and threatened by angry husbands, boyfriends and family members of women seeking help, but this...this was different. This was specific and was not about her clients at the shelter. Or at least only a fine thread connected them.

One of her clients, a Navajo woman named Doris Begay, had been living with an Anglo man, Matt Kutchner. Recently they'd left the Navajo reservation in New Mexico and moved to Durango, Colorado. Once there, Kutchner's violence escalated and Doris's daughter, Judy, had talked her mother into attending group therapy sessions at the shelter where Dulcie worked.

Dulcie had almost convinced Doris to leave the man when sixteen-year-old Judy went missing. The police questioned Dulcie about the violence she had witnessed against Judy Begay. When the young woman's battered body was found at the bottom of a mountain canyon, Dulcie's statements led to Kutchner's arrest.

But the message in her hand wasn't about the Kutchner case. It was about the questions Dulcie started asking after his arrest.

Even before her daughter's body was found, Doris had referred to her as one of the Missing Ones…almost as if she knew her daughter was dead. Since moving to Durango a year ago, Dulcie had learned about the Navajo reluctance to refer to the dead by their names. Still, the mother's use of the phrase *Missing Ones* puzzled Dulcie. How many girls were missing? When she questioned Doris, the woman grew uncomfortable and mumbled something about many reservation girls disappearing.

Dulcie's business was domestic violence. She knew the national statistics. Native American women experienced violence and exploitation at a rate ten times higher than any other ethnic group. But Dulcie did a little digging. To her shock, she discovered the number of missing girls from their area was even greater. The city's close location to multiple Native American reservations, including the massive Navajo reservation, could account for the higher numbers. But to Dulcie, the frequency of the kidnappings indicated something more…something deadly, superefficient and, so far, undetected. Could a trafficking ring be operating in the Four Corners area?

Dulcie had barely started asking questions and someone was already trying to silence her…someone who could still be outside her door.

The paper slipped through her fingers and floated to the floor. She dashed across the room and squinted

through the peephole. As far as she could see, the hallway was empty, but someone could be beyond the narrow vision of the small sight.

Threats weren't much good without force. Was someone waiting for her to step out of her apartment?

Halfway to the kitchen counter for her cell phone
she remembered something important. She'd only
discussed her concerns with two people—her boss,
Vonetta Lauder, and a municipal policeman. Officer
Shaw had been the original investigator on the Begay/
Kutchner case until they realized the victim lived outside the city limits. From that point on, jurisdiction lay
with the county sheriff's office and their detective. Still,
when Dulcie needed local statistics, she'd approached
Shaw for help. He was the only one besides her boss
who knew what she was investigating.

One of them had definitely shared the info. That
proof lay on the floor at her feet.

Vonetta was the visible representative of the domestic violence center for women, the voice of those
who couldn't speak for themselves. She sat on multiple boards, was always in the news and earned lots
of recognition and donations for the privately funded
women's center.

But Dulcie had a sense about people, a feel for their
hidden motives and agendas. She could thank her dad
for that deeply ingrained mistrust. She couldn't quite
pin down the reason she'd never trusted Vonetta, but
she'd had the same feeling about Officer Shaw. When
the Kutchner case moved to the La Plata County Sher-

iff's Office and Deputy Austin Turner, she'd felt a sense of relief.

Deputy Turner! That's who she would call. She searched her list of phone contacts for his name. She'd liked the man from the minute they met. Not just because of his appealing, boy-next-door good looks. Something about him inspired positive feelings, maybe his deep, confident voice or the lingering pain she glimpsed behind his gaze. Whatever it was, the man understood… had the same sense about people that she possessed.

During the investigation he had given her his cell number. His phone rang and rang until his message clicked on.

Dulcie licked dry lips and tried to find the right words. "Umm, Deputy Turner, this is Dulcie Parker. Can you call me as soon as possible? Something…something has happened." Her voice broke and trembled as she recited her number.

Now she would have to wait. She stared at the paper on the floor, anxiety building with each passing minute.

Don't wait. Call the sheriff's office and hunt him down.

She dialed again. The receptionist sounded busy and a little more than irritated when Dulcie asked if Deputy Turner was in.

"I don't have the answer to that, ma'am, but I can connect you to his line so you can leave a message."

"Yes. Yes please." The fear must have come through in her voice because the receptionist paused.

"Hang on. Let me see if I can find him."

The line went silent and Dulcie took several deep

breaths. Now was not the time to lose her hard-won control.

The receptionist clicked back on. "I'm sorry. He doesn't seem to be at his desk. Is there someone else I can connect you with?"

Dulcie paused. Someone else? No…she couldn't trust anyone else.

"No, thank you. I'll leave him a message."

"All right. I'll connect you."

After a short pause, Deputy Turner's deep, reassuring voice echoed in her ear again. Hearing it gave her a jolt of comfort that almost brought her to tears. "Deputy, this is Dulcie Parker. Please call me as soon as you can. It's important."

She ended the phone call, slid onto a bar stool at the counter and rested her forehead on the heels of her palms. How had she come to this again? Was she a magnet for trouble? Was her fear of being a victim creating conspiracies in her head? She looked at the paper resting on the floor.

No. This wasn't her imagination. She'd stumbled upon something deep and dark and someone was determined to keep her from exposing it.

She closed her eyes and whispered a prayer. "Please, Lord, help me."

Over and over again, she repeated the words, until the darkness threatening to overwhelm her subsided. Then she took a deep breath.

Fear was the tactic all bullies used. The only way to combat fear was to face it head-on. These people—whoever they were—wanted her to stop asking questions. That's the one thing she couldn't do. She had to move forward, had to do something.

She slid off the bar stool and walked to the door. The hallway still appeared empty. She took a deep breath and placed her ear against the door. She heard nothing. Not even another apartment door opening or the deep hum of the elevator.

No door opening. The thought stuck in her mind.

What time is it?

She glanced at her watch. Twenty minutes before eight. Every day precisely at 7:45 a.m. her neighbor across the hall left for work. Joey Delacroix worked for the city and was precise in everything he did. In five minutes on the dot, he would leave. Dulcie could leave with him.

Taking a deep breath, she swooped the paper off the ground, folded it back into the envelope and shoved it and her phone into her purse. Grabbing her coat, she slipped it on and tugged the strap of her purse over her shoulder. Then she hurried back to the door. Easing the chain out of the lock, she released the dead bolt and pressed her ear to the wooden portal again, listening for any sound.

A minute passed and her heart pounded. What if whoever left this message was waiting near the elevator? What if there were more than one? What if they weren't afraid to attack her and Joey together?

Stop it. You're letting fear overwhelm you again.

Still she needed…wanted…some way to defend herself. She looked around the room. A small can of scented aerosol spray rested on the nearby end table.

Sprayed directly in an assailant's eyes, it would make a great weapon. She popped the lid off, let it fall to the ground and gripped the can in her left hand. Then she pulled her door key out of her purse and clasped it between her fingers, pointed edge facing out.

Now she was ready. She placed her ear against the door and waited. One minute passed. Another.

Where was Joey? Had she missed him? Did he call in sick? Her pulse pounded faster with each question.

And then, the door across the hall opened. It was so loud, she shook her head and stepped back. Of course, she didn't need to press her ear against the door. Every morning she heard Joey leave while standing eight feet away in her kitchen. Fear was stealing her common sense. She needed to get control.

Straightening her spine, she tucked the aerosol can just inside her large, open purse and twisted the doorknob with fingers still clutching the key. With the door wide, she paused and glanced both directions.

All clear. She looked her neighbor's way. Joey stood motionless, his key poised just above the knob and a frown on his face.

"Hey, Dulcie. Is something wrong?"

She swallowed and stepped outside her door to lock it. "No, no. Nothing. I just… I thought I heard someone at my door earlier. Did you see anyone?"

"Nope. But I'm running a little late so I was rushing around. Might not have heard someone in the hall."

She nodded and swallowed. They locked their doors simultaneously, then walked down the hall side by side. Dulcie hesitated, waiting to see if Joey would take the elevator or the stairs. Since he was running late, maybe he'd depart from his usual choice and use the elevator. Either way, she was going the way he went.

He punched the buttons outside the elevator and turned to face her. "You sure you're okay?"

She tried to smile. "Just a lot on my mind. A busy day today."

The elevator dinged. Joey motioned for her to step in ahead of him. "Yeah, me too. We're getting close to month's end and I've got to finish a project before that."

End of October. Fall was sliding by. Cooler temperatures. Falling leaves. The golden aspens. All the russet shades and burnt oranges on the mountainsides. The colors she loved and had barely noticed this year. Life was slipping past her at the speed of light. She glanced at Joey, his pressed shirt, neat tie and overcoat. His daily "uniform." They were a lot alike. Caught up in their work, too focused to see the world around them. Maybe when all of this was over…

Dulcie looked away. Probably wouldn't happen. She had a hard time getting close to people, especially men. But one thing was certain—she was very thankful for his presence this morning. She started to tell him so when the elevator door slid open. Joey gestured for her to move ahead of him again and the moment was lost.

She paused at the front door of the apartment building, her gaze scouring the parking lot. It seemed empty, but still she hesitated. Joey reached in front of her to push the handlebar of the door.

Shaking her head, she said, "Sorry. I guess I'm not all here today."

"No problem. It's just that I'm in a bit of a hurry."

That was her cue to get moving.

The cold, brisk air made her catch her breath.

Joey moved across the lot but stood outside his car door, watching her, waiting. She hurried to her own vehicle, released the can she'd been clenching into her purse and punched the fob to unlock her door. Dulcie slid in and locked it again. Joey already had his car backed out and she watched him pull away. Then she sat in her car in the near-empty parking lot and wondered what to do next.

She couldn't go to work and face Vonetta or go to the municipal police station where Officer Shaw worked. Only one place remained where she could find help. She backed out and headed to the county sheriff's office.

Austin Turner dropped his Stetson on his desk, ran a hand through his short hair and sighed. This was one of those days when he was especially glad that as a detective, he didn't have to wear the typical county sheriff uniform. Not that he wasn't proud of the uniform. He loved the job, the work he did and most of his fellow deputies with few exceptions.

No. The job wasn't the problem. He was. For a long time now, he hadn't been able to wear the uniform with pride. Ever since the death of his Navajo wife, Abey, and their unborn child in a car accident, he hadn't felt worthy of the badge or the uniform he'd so proudly donned twelve years ago.

Again, he ran his hand through hair too short to move out of place…a nervous gesture and a sure sign that the bad feeling he'd had since waking this morning was here to stay. He'd had lots of those days in the three years since he'd lost his family. No matter how hard he tried, he couldn't shake the feeling that he should have done more. Could have prevented their deaths.

He thought he was on the mend but the brutal beating and death of a young Navajo girl had fired up all his old resentments and everything else he'd tried so hard to suppress. Many a night he'd lain awake, seeing that poor girl's body at the bottom of a mountain ravine. Those long nights ended only after he arrested the girl's stepfather.

Truth be told, the social worker involved in the case, Dulcie Parker, had contributed to his unrest. Something about the woman stuck with him. It had to be because she was so worked up…not for any other reason. There was no room in his life for another woman. Abey and his baby still filled every corner.

No, Dulcie Parker bothered him because she pushed relentlessly for answers and action. He'd only interviewed her a few times, but he never lost the feeling that she'd be following the investigation from afar, watching, waiting for results.

He recognized the bright flame of restitution in her eyes. That flame was the only thing he had in common with the redhead and was probably the one thing he didn't need in his life. After he'd struggled for so long to suppress those feelings, Dulcie fed the embers into life again…not to mention the fact that she set his nerves on edge. She was touchy and flighty, jumping away every time he got close. He didn't doubt for a moment there was a story behind those actions. She had a history, a past he didn't know and didn't want to know. The last thing he needed was a woman as close to the edge as her.

And maybe his imagination was running a marathon. He shook his head. A prolonged vacation might be the only solution to his overactive mind. He was due for some time off and his lieutenant had been pressing him to take it. The case was over. The Kutchner trial didn't start for another month, a long time from now. Until then, he needed to put all those unwanted feelings and thoughts away. Maybe he should consider some time off.

Determined to discuss the idea with his boss, he hung his hat on the rack behind him and checked the work cell phone he kept on Silent. Sleep was hard enough to attain without reporters driving him crazy all hours of the night. Since he'd arrested Kutchner, they'd been harassing him relentlessly and he needed to talk to them even less than he needed to be around Dulcie Parker.

He had a message on his phone. He hit the play button, and Dulcie's voice, the very woman he was hoping to avoid, echoed over the line. She sounded...scared. That shouldn't have surprised him. She seemed pretty uptight and easily shaken. But still her voice sounded... more than just frightened. Terrified was the right word. He released a heavy sigh. This was the last thing he wanted today, especially since she asked him to call her as soon as he could.

Fearing she had a complicating issue with the Kutchner case, he reached for his desk phone and saw the message light flashing. Dulcie was on the office machine, as well. Something was seriously wrong. Before he could even dial her number, the front desk buzzed him.

"Hey, Turner, I've got a woman here who needs to see you. She's pretty upset."

"Don't tell me. It's Dulcie Parker." He shook his head. "I guess you better send her in." He knew she was trouble from the minute he met her. There was just something about her…

He rose from his desk. The officer led Dulcie into the large common room filled with deputies' cubicles. Even across the room Austin noted her pale features— so white the red freckles across her nose and cheeks jumped out.

Taken individually, her features didn't seem to fit together. Almost black eyebrows stood out against her pale skin. They were too dark for the rest of her face, even darker than her large brown eyes. Her lips had all but disappeared in paleness. Her curly copper-shaded hair might be pretty if she didn't pull it back so tight and flat against her head. But she plastered it against her scalp and frizzy little strands rejected those tight confines. They fuzzed around her face in fiery protest.

She looked more than upset…and that meant Austin's morning would probably go from bad to worse. He stopped a few feet away and nodded. "Ms. Parker, what can I do for you?"

Glancing around, she stepped closer—but not too close, he noticed. He'd seen that action the first time they met, that she didn't let him—let anyone—get too close. In a low voice she asked, "Can we talk…someplace more private?"

Austin hesitated. Whatever she wanted, he didn't need to provide. She was toxic to him…brought feelings to life inside that were better off dead. But her colorless features and large, frightened eyes got to him. He gritted his teeth and pointed to a small room off the main area.

As soon as he closed the door, she pulled an envelope out of her purse and handed it to him. He opened it and read the message inside.

Mind your own business or you'll become a Missing One.

Austin had heard the phrase only once, at a meeting Abey had helped organize. As a member of the Navajo Nation, she had been heavily involved in multiple social organizations. In fact, he'd first met her when he was doing overtime duty at a fundraiser for Native American teens. The slender, dark-haired beauty caught his eye the minute she walked in to give an impassioned speech to the young women of her nation. At that meeting, an older Navajo woman referred to the missing and exploited Native American women by using the term *the Missing Ones*.

Over the top of the paper, Austin studied Dulcie Parker. There was a serious issue with missing and exploited Native American women. It was true, and if he'd learned anything about the woman across from him, she was the kind who would meddle in someone else's business. She wouldn't be able *not* to meddle. If he knew anything about her, it was that. Just talking to her would mean trouble for him too, trouble he was pretty anxious to avoid.

He took a slow breath. "Whose business have you been minding?"

Obviously, she didn't catch the hint of accusation in his tone. "I have no idea. All I did was ask for some statistics on missing women in the local area."

Her voice trembled. At least she had sense enough to be frightened. Maybe she'd be smart enough to walk away.

"When Doris Begay said her daughter was one of the Missing Ones…"

Austin's senses perked up. "Is this about the Kutchner case?"

"No…yes." She closed her eyes and took a slow breath. "I don't know. All I know is almost from the moment Judy disappeared Doris Begay assumed her daughter was gone forever…or dead. I'm not sure which. When I asked her why, she mumbled something about all the missing reservation girls."

Austin's jaw tightened. "So, of course, you had to check it out?"

He couldn't keep the irritation out of his tone. This time she heard the cynicism peeking through. Dark eyes, that moments ago seemed frightened and unsure, focused on him with startling clarity.

"Yes, I did. I won't turn my back on a woman or child…ever."

There it was again. The blazing passion that backed him down…backed most people down. It was a little scary. What was even more frightening… He understood that ferocious passion. He had one just like it, locked inside, eating away at his soul.

That fact hit him in the face like a slap. Dulcie Parker put him on edge because she was exactly like him…just more honest and open about it. He'd run away from his problem, even tried to hide from it. But she spoke it, walked it and lived it. If he were honest, her courage made him uncomfortable.

Ms. Parker didn't appear to notice his startled reaction. It didn't even slow her down. Now that her passion had been ignited, she was on fire. "Do you realize how many local girls are missing?"

He tried to push the thoughts away, to douse the fire with a shift of his shoulders. "We're surrounded by Native American reservations. They have the highest statistics so of course our local numbers are going to be elevated."

"Thirty-eight, Deputy Turner. Thirty-eight local women and girls have gone missing in the last three years. That's almost double the amount in the previous ten years. Even accounting for the rise in sex trafficking that's an alarming increase. Are you trying to tell me that's to be expected?"

The number *was* alarming. Why hadn't he seen that figure on any reports passing through this office? Who generated that info? Definitely something he needed to find out.

Before he could say so, she went on. "Those numbers may be acceptable to you, but they certainly are not to me."

That rankled. Was she trying to get a response out of him? Trying to ignite the same kind of angry blaze inside him? He'd been fighting for three years to keep that emotion out of his work. And now, here she was, this barely-tied-down ball of rage, trying to make him react.

She wouldn't like it if he did.

He forced himself to keep tight control. "Of course those numbers matter. There's someone's wife behind each one of them." His emotions flashed with anger. Where did she get off sounding so high and mighty? "I've never seen those stats. Where did you get your information?"

"The Durango police department. Deputy Shaw."

Shaw. Austin knew him. Most folks in the local law enforcement did. The man made sure of it. He was ambitious. Austin had worked with Shaw and frankly, he wouldn't put it past the man to try to call attention to his work any way possible. But Ms. Parker didn't know that.

"I didn't tell anyone about my research except Officer Shaw and my boss. They are the only ones who could have passed that info on to someone else to create that note."

Austin didn't know Vonetta Lauder as well as he knew Shaw, but he'd met her, watched her on the local TV programs and read about her in every newspaper in the county. Like Shaw, she seemed to enjoy the limelight. Neither of them inspired confidence in Austin. That fact alone made him willing to hear Ms. Parker out.

"Let me get this straight. Shaw gave you some kind of report?"

Some of her anger seemed to fade. "No. In fact, he wasn't tremendously helpful. He gave me a couple of internet resources that didn't tell me anything. But I'm pretty good with research. Once I got started, I found the info I needed and put the numbers together myself."

He stiffened. "You put the numbers together?"

She tensed again. "I told you. I'm good with research. Actually, excellent."

"I'm not questioning your research capabilities, Ms. Parker. Just pointing out that there's the possibility of error in your info. We all make mistakes."

She stared at him, stunned, and he watched all the spark and fire fade out of her. "You don't believe me."

"I didn't say that. It's my job to find the facts, not make dangerous guesses. Here's something else to consider. You were just involved in a high-profile murder case. Those investigations bring out the crazies and your name was all over the news. Maybe some unbalanced person or a former client decided now was the time to get back at you with this scare tactic."

She looked away. When she spoke, her voice was very low and tremulous. "It worked. I'm scared."

Austin released a frustrated sigh. "I didn't say I would not look into this. I will. I'm just trying to point out how many explanations there could be. We can't just go around jumping to conclusions, pointing fingers and naming names before we have the answers."

She gave a slight, hesitant nod. "I guess that's true." She pushed the strap of her purse higher on her shoulder and studied him, her dark eyes fathomless with strong emotions behind her tightly controlled gaze. He didn't know what they were for sure…but they were there, held in check. The intensity put him off-step.

He lifted the letter. "Can I keep this?"

She caught her breath and hesitated. For the first time, she stumbled over her words. "It's…it's the only proof I have."

Mistrust. That was the intense emotion behind her gaze. Austin's jaw tightened and his resolve hardened. "I get it. You want my help but you can't find it in yourself to trust me."

Fed up, he shoved the envelope toward her. She gripped it with shaky fingers.

Austin spun and walked toward the door. "I'll look at all this and let you know if I find anything."

She fumbled with her purse, shoved the envelope inside as she moved toward him. She paused just short of the door. "Will you…can you call me even if you find nothing? I'd like to…know."

He nodded. "I'll be in touch." He opened the door. She ducked her head and passed him, but not before he caught the defeated look on her features.

Austin followed her into the large common room and watched as she walked away. His instincts were right. She was a woman looking for a crusade and she'd triggered feelings from his convoluted past. Good police work didn't happen when the emotions were engaged. He knew that better than anyone. He needed to step back if he wanted to assess this properly…no matter how many defeated looks Ms. Parker sent his way.

He felt someone's presence behind him and turned. Lieutenant Dale McGuire, his supervisor, nudged his chin in Ms. Parker's direction. "What's she doing here?"

Austin didn't trust his own prickly attitude so he shook his head. "Nothing important."

"Good. Can I see you in my office for a minute?"

Frowning, Austin followed his lieutenant. Dale had helped him get the job here at the station. He'd been a good supervisor and a great leader. Austin liked and respected him for all those qualities.

McGuire gestured to the door. "Close that."

So…this was serious. Austin was instantly on guard. "What's going on?"

McGuire stood behind his desk. "It's pretty bizarre, that Parker woman showing up today. Not more than twenty minutes ago I got a call to watch out for her."

"Watch out. What does that mean?"

One of McGuire's eyebrows rose. Austin recognized it as his boss's "I'm not happy" signal. But what was he unhappy about? The call or Austin's questions?

He got his answer immediately. "I didn't ask questions. I just listened. You should follow my example." Dale's eyebrow still rode high on one side. "I was told that she's a troublemaker. She was fired from her last job after some scandal. Now she's looking to cash in on her claim to fame with the Kutchner case. That's the type of publicity we don't need. So back off."

Austin studied his superior. Even though he'd just had similar thoughts, it rankled to be ordered to stand down. "Since when do other people tell you how to run your staff?"

McGuire's eyebrow rose even higher. "I think what I said was to the point. I didn't ask questions and neither should you. She's trouble. Stay clear."

He picked up the file on his desk as if the conversation was over. When Austin didn't move, he looked up again.

Austin hesitated. He didn't like this. It smacked of collusion. He couldn't believe McGuire was okay with it. "Who gave you the call?"

His boss took a deep breath, obviously irritated. "Does it matter? We were advised. That's all you need to know." When Austin still didn't move, McGuire's frown deepened. "Is there something about this meeting you're not telling me?"

Dulcie said Officer Shaw was one of two people who knew about her research. Shaw belonged to the municipal police department and was a rising star. When he talked, people took notice. Did his popularity extend to the county sheriff's department too? How deep…or high did his influence go? And why was McGuire so resistant to giving Austin details about the phone call? For the first time, he questioned the motives of a man he respected and considered a friend.

"Is that an order, Lieutenant?"

His superior stiffened. "If that's how you want to take it."

"I think that's how I *have* to take it."

McGuire dropped the file to the desk. "That's fine, Turner. Take it any way you like. Just see that you do it."

Righteous senses bristling, Austin turned his back on his mentor and stalked out of the office to find Dulcie Parker's number. His boss's uncharacteristic actions just pushed him over the edge. Something was going on and Austin intended to find out what it was. Ms. Parker just became his number-one priority.

TWO

Dulcie slid behind the wheel of her car, locked the door and closed her eyes. When Judy Begay's murder investigation had been handed over to Deputy Turner, she was relieved. She'd liked the man and Dulcie couldn't say that about many people. Her background made it difficult for her to trust. But she'd had a good feeling about Deputy Turner. There had been something about him…the sense that he understood. That he was as serious about crimes against women as she was…and that he was kind. That was the most important thing. Kindness. Her early years had been dreadfully empty of that emotion. She craved it now like living water.

Her experience with Deputy Parker this morning had felt anything but that. She knew people, had strong instincts about them and was usually right. How could she have misjudged Deputy Turner so badly?

Did his boy-next-door looks turn her head, muddle her impressions? It was true he was handsome…and blond. Today was the first time she'd seen him without his cowboy hat, and she had to admit what was underneath that Stetson did not fail to appeal. He kept those golden locks short but they still had a stubborn wave in the front. His blue eyes were clear and so bright, they almost sparkled beneath the brim of his hat. He also had a cleft in his chin, a distinct little dent that set off his almost-too-pretty looks. Dulcie closed her eyes.

Okay. So…Deputy Turner's appearance had definitely made an impression and probably skewed her people instincts.

But he said he would look into it. She had to trust him and get on with her day. She reached for the key in the ignition but her fingers trembled so she couldn't grip it.

She gave her hand a shake and tried again. Still she couldn't take hold.

She was scared. Too scared to go to work and face Vonetta and too afraid to go home. She leaned back in her seat and closed her eyes. She felt like she was crossing the Grand Canyon on a tightwire with hundreds of feet of empty air beneath her. It had been a long time since she'd been this scared. Not since she and her sister hid in their closet with their arms around each other.

Her cell phone rang and she jumped a mile, bumping her knees on the wheel. Taking a deep breath, she stared at her purse. It was probably work wondering why she was late. Should she answer?

Of course she needed to answer. Otherwise they'd keep calling. On the third ring, she grabbed the purse and pulled her phone out. A sigh of relief slipped out as Deputy Turner's name flashed across the screen. She couldn't slide the on button fast enough.

"Hello?"

"Dulcie, I'm glad I caught you." His voice was pitched so low she barely heard it. "I hope you're not already at work."

Should she tell him she hadn't even left the sheriff department's parking lot? It was embarrassing, but she needed to practice trust and honesty.

"No. No, I'm not. I haven't left yet."

"Good. There's been a...development. We need to talk. But not here. I'd like to take a look at your information. Can you meet me after work...say five thirty?"

She hesitated. Did she dare invite him to her apartment? All of her files were there and he could check out her place. But that meant letting a stranger into her sanctuary. All of her old fears rose to the surface, strapping her tongue down.

"Dulcie...are you there?"

That voice. So confident. So deep and sure. She could trust him. She had to.

"Yes, I'm here. All my files are in my apartment. We can meet there."

"Great. I'll see you at five thirty, and Dulcie...I'm going to need that letter."

"Yes, yes, of course. I'll have it."

"All right. I'll see you then."

"Umm... Deputy...what should I do? I mean...if there's been a development maybe I shouldn't go to work."

He was silent for a long moment. "Do exactly what they said to do, Dulcie. Nothing. Mind your own business. Don't mention the letter, talk to anyone about it or do more research. I've got a couple of things to check on before we talk. Then I'll have a better idea of our next step."

Our next step. Dulcie sighed. That tightwire across the Grand Canyon suddenly felt like it had a safety net beneath it. She could do what she needed to do now.

"I'll see you at five thirty sharp." She gave him her address, hung up the phone and reached for the ignition key with only a slight tremor.

Austin parked on the side of the road, far down from Dulcie's apartment complex. He'd been there for almost twenty minutes watching the road. He wanted to be sure someone wasn't following Dulcie, so he waited, his fingers drumming on the wheel.

Dulcie's small white economy car came around the corner and pulled into the parking lot. Austin waited, his gaze roaming up and down the road, searching for any car that might have followed her. No vehicle stopped or even slowed. After a long while, he turned on the ignition and pulled into the driveway of the complex. Dulcie's car was parked in a spot marked with her apartment number. It looked like she was still sitting there. Was she waiting for him?

Probably. Maybe she was more sensible than he first suspected. He pulled into a visitor's space and climbed out. The night air was crisp. It would be even colder when he left. Autumn had swept into Colorado with an early storm and decided to stay. If winter followed the trend of the last few days, it would be long and cold.

He pulled out his sherpa-lined jean jacket and folded

it over his arm. Dulcie didn't leave her car until he walked up. Then the door flew open and she slid out in one smooth movement.

"Did you think I wasn't coming?"

"No, I…just didn't want to go inside by myself." She looked down, almost as if she was embarrassed to admit she was afraid. She had every right to be frightened and he felt a little guilty about his disregard this morning for the danger she seemed to be facing. Dulcie's safety was just as important as the integrity of the department. She'd just come to the wrong person for protection. He didn't feel capable of giving her a fair shake.

But she *had* come to him, and he owed her his best effort…and the same kind of honesty she now seemed determined to give him. "I was here early. I parked outside on the street to see if you were followed."

She looked up, surprise in her gaze. "Was I?"

Austin tilted his head. "No. Not from what I could see."

She sighed. "I almost wish they had followed me. That would explain how they know so much about my movements." A small breeze riffled over them like a cold breath and she shivered. "I guess we should go inside."

He gestured her forward. She lifted her purse strap higher and paused. It took her a moment, then she straightened her spine and marched ahead. She was determined even though she was afraid. He didn't know if that was bravery or foolishness. But it made Austin like Dulcie Parker just a little more.

They took the small elevator up to her apartment.

Dulcie scrambled through her large bag, looking for her keys. Just as she reached for the lock, the door across the hall opened and a man with brown hair, glasses and a full garbage bag in hand stepped out.

"Oh, hi, Dulcie." His gaze jumped from her to Austin then darted to his shoulder holster and the badge attached to his belt. Then he looked back to Dulcie. "Is everything all right?"

Her lips parted and to Austin's amazement, the woman who had no trouble expressing herself was at a loss for words.

Despite his surprise at her stalled actions, Austin stepped into the silent void for her. "No, no problem at all. Dulcie and I met a few weeks back and decided to grab a pizza some time. Tonight's the night." He smiled.

Dulcie's neighbor looked at her for confirmation. She nodded. "Joey Delacroix, this is Austin Turner. We met…a few weeks ago like he said."

A half smile, half grimace slipped over Delacroix's features. He looked so disappointed, Austin almost chuckled. Dulcie's neighbor looked back at him and Austin smiled, the biggest, most self-satisfied grin he could manage. "Nice to meet you."

Austin held out his hand. Joey grasped it, then the man looked away quickly. "Yeah…same here. See you later."

He gripped the bag and scooted down the hall like he was embarrassed. Puzzled by the encounter, Austin looked at Dulcie for an explanation. But she ducked her head and opened the door.

Was his arrival interfering with a budding romance?

Did this mousey guy, who seemed afraid of his own shadow, know anything about his neighbor? His impression of Dulcie was of a driven woman who took no prisoners and left no one behind in her quest for justice for abused women. Mousey guy didn't have a chance. Austin didn't even try to stifle his pleasure at the thought.

He followed Dulcie inside, oddly pleased. Not that he had…or even wanted a claim on Ms. Parker. He just didn't think Delacroix should have one either.

Pushing aside his wayward thoughts, Austin surveyed the room. Dulcie crossed to the kitchen bar and set down her bag. The living room was meticulously clean. Furnished with a serviceable brown sofa and chair with a glass-topped table in between. It looked like standard apartment issue. But Dulcie had added her own splashes of color. Blue-and-green pillows and the same colors in a swath of material above the blinds. A soft, comfy-looking blue beanbag chair rested in one corner of the room beside a small, glass-topped desk. Paper files were stacked on top. Nothing was out of place. It almost felt too organized, too straight and neat…like the woman nervously looking around her home. But to his surprise, Austin found the room welcoming. He could sit on the couch and stay for a while. As much as he loved his own cabin on the mountain, it didn't have this "get comfortable" feeling.

He studied Dulcie as she slid out of her coat. "This is nice. You've made this small place feel…homey."

She sent him a shy, pleased smile. "Thank you. I'm not here much but when I am, I want it to be comfortable, you know? I'm glad somebody else likes it too."

She took his hat and coat from him, careful not to let their hands touch, and hung them both on a stand near the door. Austin couldn't resist teasing her just a little. "Did I just destroy a blossoming romance?"

"What? Of course not!" The pink tinge that came into her cheeks told him otherwise. Not to mention the fact that she refused to look him in the face. When she finally glanced up, he lifted his eyebrows in a question.

She sighed. "Really. I've barely spoken to the man. It's just…well, he walked me to the elevator this morning and I felt a little thankful. That's all."

Austin chuckled, almost to himself. "If you say so."

He lifted the blinds and checked the locks. No marks or spots where the window might have been jimmied. He peeked outside, saw that there was no balcony or a ledge wide enough to crawl along. Then he examined the door frame, searching for evidence of an attempt to pry the door open. At last, he tested the handle and found it sturdy and tight.

"Can I check the bedroom?"

"Sure." She sounded confident but scooted down the hall ahead of him. He didn't know what she was so nervous about. The bedroom was in the same meticulous order as the living room. Windows secure. Closet doors shut. But he checked inside anyway, just to reassure her.

"Everything is good, Dulcie. It doesn't look like anyone even attempted to get inside. Just keep the locks on and do your laundry in some public place. No dark basement rooms until we get this sorted out."

She nodded. "I will. Thank you."

He headed back down the hall. As he passed the

bathroom, a soft scent drifted toward him. Flowery and green like grass or broken leaves. It reminded him of a soft spring evening. He liked it. Was it Dulcie's perfume or some sort of room deodorizer? If she let him get closer to her than three feet, he might know the answer. But every time they got anywhere near each other, she skittered away like a wild animal. He hesitated just a moment longer, taking in the pleasing aroma, but she halted, three feet behind him. What happened to the "no prisoners taken" woman? Was she only fearless when she was protecting other women and children? Shaking his head, he moved forward.

Back in the living room, he went straight to the desk. "Are these files your research?"

"Yes. Take a look while I order us a pizza. Can I get you something first…a soda or a bottle of water?"

"Yeah. I'd like a soda if you have it."

She picked up the cell phone and dialed. While she waited for an answer, she walked to the fridge and came back with a cola. "What kind of pizza?"

"Anything with meat."

He looked at the files on the desk. Each of them was at least an inch thick. She had four full folders. If she had done all of this on her own in such a short time, she *was* an excellent researcher. He carried the files to the sofa and plopped down. It was as comfortable as it looked. He'd had a long, tense day trying to avoid his lieutenant and keep busy. All he wanted right now was to lean back on Dulcie's front-room sofa, rest his head on the soft blue pillow and close his eyes. But the files lay heavy in his arms.

He opened the first and began to read. Name after name. Place after place. Most of the missing women had home addresses on the reservations. Not a good thing since all of those places were out of his jurisdiction. In order to start any kind of investigation, he'd have to ask permission and cross official lines. That by itself would be difficult.

The doorbell rang. Dulcie, who had taken the chair at the end of the sofa—as far from him as she could get—tensed. She was still frightened and since she was already uptight and determined not to get too close to him, this whole situation was looking bleak.

Austin shook his head and rose. She hurried after him and stood behind him. Austin took the pizza box from the delivery boy. Dulcie reached around him to hand the college kid a wad of money. Austin shut the door and reached for his wallet. "Here, let me…"

"Absolutely not. This is my treat. You don't know how much I appreciate this."

Austin studied her downcast features. There it was again. That little tremor of fear in her voice. She must have heard it too, as a wash of pink flushed over her cheeks. She seemed ashamed of her fear, embarrassed by it. She had every reason to be afraid and no reason to be ashamed.

He handed her the pizza and, with new resolve, went back to the files, searching for a common thread between the missing women. Dulcie brought him a piece of pizza on a paper plate. He reached up and cupped one hand under hers to support the plate. Her soft skin sent a jolt through his fingertips before she jerked away.

Had she felt that little electric charge? He looked up into her startled gaze.

"Sorry. I'm still jumpy."

Right…and her nerves were contagious. He was beginning to feel as tense as she acted. How were they going to work together if they made each other feel like cats walking on hot tin roofs?

He turned away, tried to focus on the files beneath him. It worked. Soon, he was lost in the names, dates and places. Dulcie had already separated the cases by years, three to be exact. Roughly ten women each year, living in different locations, had disappeared. But the staggered dates and locations of the disappearances had perfect precision, as if they were planned out months in advance. These were not crimes of opportunity, but were systematic. Austin's insides tightened as that truth sank in. These people were smart, powerful and deadly…and he had no clue how to penetrate their web.

But he was only skimming the files. He had to go deeper.

"We need to tear these files apart. We need pencils and paper." After such a long silence, his words startled Dulcie and she dropped her pizza slice onto her lap. She peeled it off and flopped it on the paper plate, but a large spot of red sauce covered her black pant leg.

"Oh no." She wiped the stain with a napkin then rose quickly and hurried to the desk. She brought two yellow legal pads and a pile of pencils back to the coffee table. "I'll be right back. I have to change."

Austin nodded, grabbed one pad and jumped back into the first file. By the time she returned, he was deep into dates and barely glanced up when she entered the room. When he did, he almost dropped his pencil.

She'd changed into a long-sleeved top over stretchy workout pants. There was nothing particularly flattering about the outfit except the color. The purple toned down all the harsh carroty tinge of her freckles and turned her lips to the color of peaches. And her hair… Those orange wisps around her face had disappeared into curls the color of burnished copper that fell in glossy coils well below her shoulders. Brows that had seemed too large and too full now matched the deep brown of her eyes and the dark fire in her hair. She looked wild, barely contained and completely unfathomable.

He was staring. Knew he was staring but couldn't stop. Dulcie Parker was beautiful. She looked uncomfortable beneath his scrutiny. He tried to gather his thoughts and felt like he needed to apologize. For what, he didn't know.

"I'm sorry," he said at last. "It's just you look…so different."

"I know. My hair always seems to get lots of unwanted attention. That's why I usually pull it back."

Unwanted. Austin shook his head as understanding sank deep inside him. In one sentence, she'd hit upon the source of their tense relations. "It shouldn't be unwanted, Dulcie. A beautiful woman shouldn't be afraid to be beautiful."

He didn't dare look up to see what impact his probably "unwanted" observation might have on her. He was afraid if he looked up, he'd tell her how her hair was like a crown and made everything else fit into place. But he knew she wouldn't appreciate the compliment so he kept his gaze on the files in front of him.

"How did things go at work today?"

"Good." She cleared her throat. "It went better than I thought. Vonetta's attending a conference and won't be back for three days."

"No one else asked any questions? Nothing seemed suspicious or out of order?"

"Not at all. If I hadn't found that letter under my door, it would have been a perfectly normal day."

He nodded and finally dared to look up. "Well, my day was anything but normal. Someone sent an order to my lieutenant suggesting that I stay away from you."

Dulcie slumped to the chair at the end of the sofa. "Someone warned you to stay away from me?"

"Yeah, before you even arrived at the station."

She stared at him, stunned. "How did they know…" Words seemed to slip away from her and fright built on her features. "Is that why you called me? To let me down easily and tell me you can't be involved?"

His lips tilted upward. "Not likely. I don't take those kinds of orders."

Dulcie's lips parted in what seemed like relief and she swallowed. Her fire-wrapped hair framed her neck, made it appear long, white and incredibly soft. Once again, he felt himself staring.

She walked to the desk, pulled out another file and handed it to him.

"What's this?"

"It's important. I need you to read it."

He opened the file. It was an employment report

from Dulcie's last job in California. A mother came to the shelter with a split lip and bruises, an obvious victim of domestic abuse. But it was her little girls who caught Dulcie's attention. She'd kept a tight record of their responses. The sisters showed no signs of violence and made no comments. In fact, they refused to speak, shied away from the touch of anyone…just like Dulcie. Obviously, their actions ignited her concerns. When the woman weakened and returned to her husband, Dulcie broke all her counseling boundaries and pushed the mother to the point of harassment. She resorted to waiting outside the woman's house and following her, begging her to return to the shelter. Eventually, the husband discovered Dulcie's presence and filed a complaint. Her supervisors had no choice but to let her go.

Austin looked up. Dulcie watched him with those dark, unfathomable eyes. What was behind that unreadable gaze? What did she want him to say?

It didn't really matter what *she* wanted. He had one very important question. "Did you convince the mother to return?"

She swallowed again. "No. I heard later that she ended up in the hospital and the father disappeared… with the two little girls. They haven't been seen since."

Austin looked down. Anger rushed through him. Once again he felt that ruthless, vicious rage that he worked so hard to contain. He'd been right. Dulcie Parker wasn't good for him. Her past, her present— everything about her—ignited his banked rage.

He lifted the file. "You didn't have to show me this."

She nodded slowly. "Yes…I did. Because there's one

more thing you should know." She licked dry lips. "I'm
not so sure I won't do it again…cross the line, I mean.
I couldn't live with myself if I lost more little girls."

All the passion inside Austin froze. She was talking
about herself and didn't know she'd just put his own unspoken emotions into words. He couldn't live with himself if he lost something—someone—else, including a
copper-headed woman with dark passion hiding behind
her gaze.

The thought of Dulcie endangering herself, continu-
ing to put her job and maybe even her life in danger for
these women made his instincts flare like live wires. He
dropped the file down on the table. "I hope you mean
that because it looks like you've already put your life
on the line."

Dulcie stiffened as Austin slammed the file shut. A
frown creased the spot between his eyebrows and when
he was angry, that little cleft in his chin twitched. She'd
noticed it before, almost the first time they'd met when
he was questioning her about Judy Begay and her relationship with her stepfather. That little twitch was a
sign for Dulcie. Austin might try to act like he didn't
care, but he did…deeply, and for that reason, his anger
didn't frighten her.

He raised a tense gaze to hers and lifted the folder
again. "It also says in here you handled twenty-five
cases in the three years you worked with this shelter.
They gave you this file and made a point of saying how
well you had performed before this incident. That tells

me they wanted to help you any way they could. What happened, Dulcie? Why did this case make you snap?"

She took a deep breath. "The two little girls reminded me of my sister and me."

It was hard to talk about it. But she had to tell him. She needed to make him understand. "My dad was a well-respected professor, a very popular teacher. But at home he was a monster. Anytime something fell short of perfection, he took it out on my mother. My sister and I would hide in our closet. Then one day my sister spoke up and he knocked her across the room."

Dulcie swallowed. "As soon as he left for work, my mother packed our bags. I remember her hands trembling the whole time. We took a taxi to a shelter. They helped my mother file a restraining order. Then they found her a job and gave us counseling. I wouldn't be here if not for that shelter. That's why I do what I do. I wouldn't have a life if not for someone who cared enough to be there."

His voice was low and maybe still angry. "So now you have to be that person. The one who cares."

She nodded. "I worked hard to have a normal life, to overcome my fears and walk in the world with my head held high. I thought I was over my past. But that encounter with the little girls, and now this letter… They both sent me spiraling back again. They made me feel like a helpless child and I don't like that feeling."

Austin looked at the file, avoiding her gaze. But his jaw clenched and a muscle twitched. He didn't like what was happening any more than she did. That assuaged her fear.

"I know you care, Dulcie. You didn't have to show me this." He lifted the file.

She licked her lips and shook her head. "That's not why I gave it to you. I just wanted you to know it's not personal. I…I have a hard time trusting people, but I do trust you…as much as I'm able. Do you understand?"

He leaned back on the sofa and was silent for a long while. "Yes, I think I do."

He placed his elbows on his knees and linked his fingers. He had strong hands. They looked like they could handle anything. They made her feel safe. *He* made her feel safe. That was a new and startling feeling. She had a hard time growing close to anyone, and feeling secure with someone was way out of her experience. Austin Turner was sending her down new paths.

His amazing, strong jaw tightened even more, making the cleft twitch. "Look, I'm not going to lie to you. I didn't want to get involved. I still don't. My wife was a part of the Navajo Nation. I…"

His voice broke and he looked away. "I lost her and my unborn child to a drunk driver three years ago. I came here to get away. The last thing I want is to get involved in anything like this."

Shock waves swept over Dulcie. She didn't know he had suffered such a loss, and from the look on his face, he was still suffering. Three years and he was still in pain. She should have known, should have recognized that kind of pain, the kind of fear that held one back and kept a normal life in check. And yet, another very strong emotion had pushed him out from behind that wall. What was it?

"Why *did* you get involved? Why did you agree to help me?"

He looked up and his blue-eyed gaze was as cold as steel. "The fact that someone in the force is using their power to keep you quiet. I won't stand by and let corruption tear down the department. The men I've worked with… Most of them are good officers, good men. Whoever is behind this needs to be stopped. I won't let them destroy the only thing I still care about."

She took a deep breath. "I understand. I never thought I'd work in social services again. I was certain I'd end up a clerk in some government office. Vonetta knew my history, the whole story and hired me anyway. I was so thankful for the second chance, but now I'm right back in the same place. I've crossed a line I didn't even know was there."

Austin was silent for a moment. "Did you ever think there's a possibility Vonetta hired you because of your past?"

"What do you mean?"

"Anyone who has met you knows you're passionate about the women you serve. She probably suspected you would cross lines again and that willingness would make you the perfect person to blame if things went wrong."

Cold trickled through Dulcie and she stared at him.

"Don't look so surprised. These people, whoever they are, are powerful. They got my boss to warn me off and he's one of the most upright men I know. Their plans are complicated, like a web. A group this organized probably has contingency plans for everything, especially the future."

Dulcie was stunned. "You don't really think she hired me because I'd be easy to blame, do you?"

He shrugged. "My gut says this group is powerful and smart. I want to move carefully. And I need that letter."

Dulcie didn't hesitate. She grabbed it from her purse and handed it to him.

Austin nodded his head in approval. "We've had our fingers all over it. I doubt the lab will find anything besides our prints, but it's the only solid clue we have. I'll get it to a friend and see if she can't put a rush on it."

That little cleft in his chin twitched as his jaw tightened. He gestured to the files on the table. "Most of these cases involve multiple justice departments, the municipal police, the county sheriffs and the Navajo police. Jurisdictions cross and recross. The tribal police have no authority off the reservation and the municipal police have none on tribal lands. Add the FBI and their particular duties to the mix and you have a fouled-up system. This group has taken advantage of that fact."

He shook his head. "I'm not sure how much help I can be. In the first year only two victims lived in my jurisdiction. No telling how many others are outside my boundaries. I can pull those two reports without drawing attention but asking for others might send up red flags—flags we don't need flying."

He picked up the first year's file. "And…I don't know how we can connect Officer Shaw. I haven't found a link to him, but someone in law enforcement is involved otherwise my boss wouldn't have tried to pull me off. Who knows how far up the chain of command it goes? Not to mention all the other questions we have to answer. How do they operate? Do they hold their victims in the local area or move them immediately? How do they transport them? But most of all, we need to find those first connections. How are these girls chosen? What place or people do they have in common and what sets them up to be targets?"

Dulcie shook her head. "That's the one thing I've been going over and over in my mind. Judy Begay had a best friend, Susan, from her days on the reservation. The two girls met every Friday at a bar. I always wondered how her stepfather found their meeting place. I could never get that info out of Judy."

Austin stared at her. "What are you talking about? There's nothing in the report about Judy meeting with another girl the night she disappeared."

"Judy rushed out of the center to meet Susan. I told Officer Shaw…"

They stared at each other—silent—until Austin shook his head. "Shaw left a very important detail out of his report so that puts him back at the top of the suspect list." His features darkened. "And that puts my whole case against Kutchner in jeopardy. We might have the wrong man in jail."

Dulcie shivered. Austin's features were frozen. He was coldly, silently furious. His job, the men he worked with, meant a lot to him and this betrayal went deep. Dulcie respected his feelings, even admired them. But somehow, she was a little disappointed. Had some deep, unspoken part of her wished Austin had agreed to help for her sake? Was her initial trust of Austin based on something else…those handsome all-American looks and a dimple that telegraphed his feelings? Was she attracted to him?

Of course not. Her instincts wouldn't betray her like that. She respected and admired his devotion. And of course, she felt compassion for his loss. He was a complicated man who intrigued her. That was all. Nothing more.

"Do you have any clues about the location of the bar?" His question drew her attention back to the issue at hand.

"No, I asked Judy multiple times, but she wouldn't tell me. The topic just slipped out one day when she was talking about Susan. They'd been friends since they were little."

"All the more reason why Susan should have been included in the investigation. Do you have a last name?"

"No, I'm sorry. If Judy said it, I don't remember."

"Well, we're going to have to find this girl. I have something I have to do tomorrow morning, but first chance I get, I'll question Doris Begay again."

Dulcie bit her lip. "She's not here. She moved back to the reservation when Matt Kutchner was arrested."

"It figures." Austin flopped back on the sofa and rubbed his face. "What's tomorrow?"

"Friday."

Apparently, his mind was starting to drag with fatigue. He shook his head. "Look, it's late and I'm tired.

I need to tackle this fresh in the morning." He gathered the files into a pile.

He was leaving. Actually leaving. The thought of being alone in her apartment ignited her trepidations. "What…what shall I do tomorrow?"

He gave a quick shake of his head. "The same thing. Nothing. No questions. No research at work. Act like you are doing exactly what they want."

She gestured to the files and her hand trembled slightly. She dropped it quickly, hoping Austin didn't see the telltale shaking. "Why don't you leave those with me? I'll break them down for you."

"Are you sure? We need a lot of information culled out of them."

"I will not sleep anytime soon. I might as well make the time productive."

He studied her for a moment then nodded. "All right. Make separate lists for each year. Write down anything the cases have in common, names, places, friends, anything that doesn't seem right. We'll go over the lists tomorrow night when we meet again."

He started to stand then paused. "You'll be all right, won't you?"

Studying his weary features, she stomped on her jumping nerves and nodded. "I'll be fine."

"Okay." He stood, slid his Stetson into place, grabbed his coat and headed for the door. "Remember, keep a low profile tomorrow and call me if something comes up."

"I will. I promise."

He hesitated for one moment, then unlocked the dead

bolt and opened the door. The minute he stepped out and closed it, Dulcie twisted the lock and slid the chain into place. Then she stood there, listening to his footsteps as he walked down the hall. After everything had gone silent, she finally stepped away from the door. Her knees were a little weak. She plopped down on the couch and closed her eyes.

Lord, I need to be strong. Need to help Austin. I need Your strength.

She spoke her favorite scripture out loud until her fear began to fade.

"And that he might make known the riches of his glory on the vessels of mercy, which he had afore prepared unto glory."

Riches of His glory He had prepared for her. She was unique and beloved of God. Her father had not valued and treasured her, but God did. He'd prepared riches for her even before she was born. One of them was her normal life. After the horror of her early childhood, her day-to-day living held a certain peace and was a blessing. The fact that she could be of service to other beaten and beleaguered women was another richness. They were His promises fulfilled, what He had prepared for her. She'd believed that for most of her life.

But for the first time, when she spoke the scripture, she felt uneasy…felt a question forming. First the woman and her daughters in California. Now this threat. Were these incidents God's way of telling her she was on the wrong path?

She shook her head. That couldn't be the source of her unrest. She was certain she was meant to fight for those who couldn't. That conviction filled her entire being. Something else was causing this unrest, but she couldn't put her finger on it.

Prayer would answer her question soon enough. In the meantime, she needed to get to work. She pulled her fluffy throw off the back of the couch, wrapped it around her and opened the first file.

She worked for hours. It wasn't until she'd gone through all three years of paperwork that she finally put the pencil down, leaned into the pillow and closed her weary eyes.

She didn't open them again until her alarm woke her the next morning. The buzzer was going nonstop in the bedroom. She glanced at her watch. The alarm had gone off at least a half an hour ago. She'd be late to work if she didn't get moving.

Throwing off the blanket, she dashed to the shower and dressed in record time. She didn't even try to do makeup. Pulling her wet hair back into a tight bun, she grabbed a protein bar from the kitchen and made it to the front room just as she heard Joey's door open across the hall.

Sliding the chain loose, she twisted the lock and opened the door. Joey paused. "Good morning. I guess we're on the same timetable again today."

She gave him a hesitant smile. "Barely. I didn't hear my alarm."

"Is everything okay? You look a little…frazzled."

"Oh, yeah. Everything's fine. I just hate being late."

She locked the door and headed to the elevator. Joey filed in right behind her. Downstairs, he opened the

glass door for her, and she smiled again, this time trying to appear more confident. Her car was close by and
she pulled her keys out as Joey strode across the lot to
his. She waved, beeped her lock, then looked down at
her handle.

The words *No Cops* were scratched into the paint
just above it.

She froze for one long minute. Then her gaze shot
around the parking lot.

"Are you sure you're okay?"

Joey stood outside his car, the door open. Dulcie
swallowed hard and nodded. "Yes, everything's fine."

She slid in, jammed the key into the ignition and
drove away. She waited until she was far down the road
before she pulled over and dialed Austin's number.

He didn't answer. His voice message came on. Just
hearing his voice gave her the encouragement she
needed to keep from falling apart. "Austin, it's me,
Dulcie. I know you said you didn't see anyone following me, but there has to be someone watching me. They
know we met last night. The words *No Cops* were keyed
into my car this morning." Her voice cracked and she
was silent for a long time while the message kept running. At last, she found her voice. "All right. I'm going
to work. Call me when you get this."

THREE

Lieutenant McGuire had sent Austin a text late last night asking him to come in early. Austin was right on time. Five in the morning was one of the few hours during the day when the station was quiet. The emptiness of the place, with no one loitering in the office area and no phones ringing, increased Austin's tension. Not to mention the fact that he hadn't slept well. With Dulcie's information and concern for how to deal with McGuire swimming around in his head, he'd tossed and turned most of the night. He marched straight to the break room for a mug of coffee. Sipping the hot liquid, he let it burn its way down his throat, hoping it might clear away the foggy fumes of frustration.

Dulcie's research had struck a nerve with someone… a person with a lot of pull in the force. That kind of power was bad for the department and bad for the men he worked with. He needed to find out who was pulling the strings and why. The only place he could start was here. McGuire's light was on in his office.

Picking up his coffee mug, Austin headed to meet

his supervisor. The last thing he wanted was to create a break between him and a man he considered a friend, but it had to be done. He knocked on the door frame. "You wanted to see me."

Seated at his desk, McGuire gestured Austin in. "Close the door behind you."

Austin obeyed and stood in front of the desk. Every muscle in his body tensed as his mind desperately searched for a way to wiggle the information he needed out of his boss.

McGuire handed him an envelope. "The search warrant for the Carson place came through late yesterday."

Mrs. Carson and her son lived in the San Juan Mountains just south of Silverton. Unfortunately, Mrs. Carson's property fell within the La Plata County boundaries, so Austin's team had inherited the case. Mrs. Carson and her thirty-year-old son were estranged because of his long history of crime. Unfortunately, during a good time in their relationship, Mrs. Carson had allowed him to move into a remote cabin on the edge of her acreage. However, their relationship soured again. She'd filed a report claiming he had threatened her and was using her cabin as a holding place for stolen property. Austin suspected Carson had already cleared out.

He took the envelope from McGuire. "You know this is probably a waste of time. Do you want me to handle it this morning?" He dreaded hearing the answer. The drive to the Carson property would take most of the day. He didn't want to go that far from Dulcie.

"Yes, and I've called Bolton and Cornell in early to go with you. It could get ugly."

Austin nodded and stalled, searching for a way to broach the subject creating such turmoil inside him.

McGuire beat him to it. "Listen, about our conversation yesterday."

Austin froze. "Sir?"

"I handled it badly. I was angry and I took it out on you. I don't enjoy conversations where a superior talks down to me, like I don't know how to handle my own men. And then, when I walked out and saw Ms. Parker here, it put me over the edge." He leveled his gaze on Austin. "I've never taken orders from anyone about my men…and I will not start now. You have my permission to ignore the instructions I gave you yesterday."

"You don't know how glad I am to hear that, sir."

The lieutenant had strong features, short brown hair streaked with white strands and a broad nose. One dark eyebrow rose in a tilted quirk. "I suspected there was more to that meeting than you mentioned. Anything you want to talk about?"

Austin hesitated. "Only if you want to tell me who issued the warning."

"Done. It came straight from the district attorney as a 'courtesy call.' One official to another from DA Havlicek. He did everything he could to convince me that Ms. Parker was trouble. Said she was fired from her last job and not to be trusted. I don't care about her employment record and his call was so far out of line I could barely control myself. Ordinarily I would have told him just what I thought of his 'courtesy call,' but I held my tongue. Something's going on and I want to know what it is."

Austin was more than relieved McGuire felt the same way he did about the call. He only hoped his lieutenant would feel the same way about his other suspicions.

"You're right. Something is going on." He told his lieutenant everything Dulcie had relayed to him, right down to the statistics on the Native American women.

McGuire agreed with Austin's assessment. "I've seen some high numbers but, like you, assumed our location was the common factor. Those numbers might have gone unnoticed until Ms. Parker pushed and someone pushed back."

"My thoughts exactly."

"First thing you need to do is find out from Ms. Parker what the DA has on her. It could turn into something we don't want associated with this department."

Austin nodded. "I already did. They fired her from her last job for pressuring a client to come back to the safety of the shelter where she worked."

McGuire's eyebrow rose again. "That's tough."

"Yeah and now, barely a year into this new job, she stumbles across what looks like a sex-trafficking ring."

His supervisor's gaze jumped up. "You think it's that serious? Not just a couple of opportunistic grabs?"

"No way, sir. These guys are smart. They've got plans and—as you witnessed—pull. I didn't take Dulcie's story too seriously until you gave me that order. Then I knew powerful people are behind this. The DA, Officer Shaw and Ms. Lauder, they carry weight in this town."

McGuire agreed. "I've known Vonetta Lauder a long time. She's an ambitious woman with an agenda. I've never figured out exactly what that agenda is, but I don't think her whole heart is in her work." He shook his head abruptly. "We need to keep a tight lid on this. If I take you away from your other duties, someone might ask questions we're not ready to answer. Until we know who we can trust, you need to look like you're working your other cases. I'll cover for you as much as I can, but I want this to be your top priority. We have to sort this out quickly and quietly."

Austin nodded. "So, I'm still heading up the mountain to the Carson place?"

"Yes, this has been your case. If I hand it off to someone else, it will look bad. Take care of that today, then we'll see what we can do about freeing you. I might even need to order you to take some time off." McGuire smiled a wry grin. "I've been trying to convince you to do that. Now it'll be an order even if this vacation wasn't the kind I had in mind."

Austin grinned. "Keeping busy. My kind of rest."

McGuire motioned him toward the door. "Get out of here and get back as quickly as you can. In the meantime, I'll see if I can check in to a connection between Lauder and the DA."

Austin gave him a mock salute and headed out, feeling better than he had since Dulcie walked into the department. He left a message for Bolton and Cornell to meet him at a coffee shop on the way out of town. Then he grabbed his jacket and drove to the lab. His friend Cindy had done some expedited work for him before. He hoped he could convince her to make Dulcie's letter a priority. She agreed and Austin was back on the road in a heartbeat. By the time Bolton and Cornell arrived at the shop, he had coffee for them ready and waiting to go.

They headed up the mountain with the sun tipping over the high peaks and casting a warm, golden glow over the roads and trees. Austin had a hard time focusing on the work ahead of him. All he could think about was Dulcie's predicament. But he needed to get on track. This warrant for the Carson place might be a run-of-the-mill job, but McGuire was right. Bob Carson was dangerous, and Austin needed to be mentally prepared.

He tried to call Mrs. Carson and let her know they were on their way, but he'd waited too long. He'd lost cell service this high on the mountain.

The Carson house was even farther up, almost five miles off the main road, at the end of a bumpy, dusty trail. As soon as they pulled into the drive of the dilapidated house, Mrs. Carson came out to greet them. She told him the warrant had taken too long. Her son had been gone from the cabin for over a week and he was keeping company with Walter Benally. Austin knew the man well. He was a hard case. Five years in prison. Damaged vocal cords from a prison fight. Multiple assault charges after he was released. He worked for Johnny Whitehorse at his bar just outside the Navajo reservation…a dangerous gathering place for all the local criminal element. At one time, every thief, robber and drug dealer in the Four Corners area passed through Whitehorse's place called *The Round Up*. As far as Austin was concerned, Bob Carson had just taken a step up on the criminal food chain ladder.

Austin and his men traveled farther up the dirt road. The cabin was empty and vandalized. Carson had done serious damage to his mother's place before he left. It had broken windows with trash strewn about, but one thing struck Austin as unusual. A large O-shaped ring was screwed into the wall above one of the dirty mattresses on the floor. The heavy-duty ring didn't budge even when he slammed his foot against it. He couldn't figure out a reason or a purpose for the metal ring.

With nothing else to find, Austin and his men left the ramshackle cabin. Bolton and Cornell drove on down the mountain. Austin stopped to talk to Mrs. Carson and have her sign the paperwork. When she finished, he said, "If your son comes back, just let us know."

"I won't be here if he does. I'm moving to Florida with my sister. So he'll be your problem…or the new owners'."

"You're selling the place?"

"Already had an offer from Rocky Mountain Dreams, that big realty company in Silverton. They told me they had someone willing to buy it for more than I hoped for."

Austin's uncle Butch was a locomotive engineer who worked on the narrow-gauge railroad based in Silverton. They ran the old-time steam engines up and down the mountain from the mining-town-turned-tourist-center to Durango. His uncle had talked about the owner of Rocky Mountain Dreams, Kent Pierce, and his control of the town's chamber of commerce. Uncle Butch even suggested that Pierce had shady connections with the police department. Austin thought of the cabin, the mys-

terious ring and wondered if Pierce could have any connection with Benally and Carson. He didn't have enough
info to put all the pieces together but his investigative
instincts had flashed on to high alert.

But for now, he needed to get back to town and Dulcie. With one last glance at Mrs. Carson's retreating
back, he hurried to his vehicle and headed down the
mountain. The image of Dulcie's trembling fingers flit-
ted through his mind. She had a way of tugging on one
of her curls, winding it around her finger when she was
upset. She'd done that almost the whole time they were
together last night.

The image stuck in his mind because it was a mea-
sure of her fear…not for any other reason. Most definitely not because she had that wild woman/frightened
child look about her. If—and that was a big if—he were
to take interest in a woman, it wouldn't be one like Dulcie with her deep-seated fears. No. He wanted another
warrior woman like Abey. But there wasn't anyone like
his wife. She was one of a kind and any thoughts about
Dulcie were based on concern. She needed help. That
was all. Even if he wasn't the right person for the job,
he couldn't resist helping someone in danger.

Shaking his head, he pushed the speedometer as he
hurried back to town. The minute he had reception, his
cell phone buzzed with messages, three in a row. The
first was from Dulcie. He was out of reception when
she called, so he'd missed it. First chance, he pulled off
to the side of the road and listened.

*Austin, it's me, Dulcie. I know you said you didn't
see anyone following me, but there has to be someone*

watching me. They know we met last night. The words No Cops *were keyed into my car this morning.*

He'd been so careful. He was certain no one was watching her. How had the gang found out they had met?

She'd sent him a second message around one that afternoon. *Hey, it's me again. I...I haven't heard from you so I'm a little worried. I'm at work, but I can't concentrate. I'm going home early and locking the door behind me. Call when you get this.*

Good. That was the safest place for her until he could get there. He had one last message and punched the button. It was Cindy from the lab.

Hey, you owe me a coffee. That letter was handled so much the prints were overlapping, but I found one on the inside of the envelope. It's a partial, but I'm confident I've got the right guy. His prints are on file because he works for the city. His name is Joey Delacroix.

Cindy kept talking, but Austin didn't hear a word she said.

Joey Delacroix. Dulcie's neighbor right across the way. The mousey guy she was so thankful had walked her to her car. He was the one sending her threatening messages and watching her every move right out her front door...and she was headed home again...straight into his arms. Austin had to warn her.

Dulcie pulled into her complex's parking lot and closed her eyes. Thankfully it was a Friday and she'd been able to get away early. Not as early as she'd hoped but still...she didn't think she could take another hour of trying to look normal when her insides were sloshing around like liquid.

She pulled out her phone. Still no call from Austin. She knew he was busy, but he'd said to call him. He promised to help but almost seven hours later…no response. Something was wrong.

But she couldn't just sit in her locked car and wait for him. She needed to get inside her apartment. Once there, she'd be safe, and she'd call the department and ask for him. There was only one problem… Getting to her apartment.

Carefully, she checked the cars in the parking lot. All were empty. She noticed that Joey's car was in its usual place. He was home early today too. That made her feel a little better.

One hand grasped her phone, the other twisted her keys in her usual "punch" grip, one key pointed out. Then she jerked open the door, hit the lock button and dashed for the apartment entrance. She ran through the empty entry to the elevator. The doors closed behind her. She sighed with relief. When they opened, the hall was empty too. She hurried toward her door, fumbling to get the right key out of the "punch" hold.

Just as she reached her place, Joey's door opened. She jumped but pressed a hand to her thumping heart at the sight of her friendly neighbor. "You startled me."

"Sorry. I've been hoping to catch you. I'm glad you came home early today."

She gave him a half-hearted smile. "Yes, I was feeling a little off and it was a slow day. How about you? Why are you off so early on this Friday?"

"I'm about to close the door on a very long project so I thought I'd celebrate."

"Really? That sounds like a fun evening."

He stepped closer. "Actually, I was hoping you'd join me. I mean…well, I wanted to give you time to get settled, but you've been here a year now and well…I just thought…" He hesitated. "The truth is your deputy friend was here last night and well…I'd like to put my hat in the ring if you're looking for…pizza-night friends."

Stunned, Dulcie stared at him. "I—I wasn't exactly looking for…friends."

"No, of course not. I put that badly. I just meant I'd like to spend more time with you. I thought we could start tonight. Something simple. Just a quick drink to celebrate my success."

Tonight. Three days ago, even two days ago, she'd have jumped at the chance but tonight… No way was she going out.

"I'm sorry, Joey. Not tonight. I'm a little under the weather. That's why I came home early."

He stepped even closer. "Please, Dulcie. It would mean a lot to me. We can stay in. I'll bring over the drinks. I have everything. You name it—I've got it."

His plea sounded so heartfelt. If it meant that much to him…maybe she could make it work. After all, he'd helped her. She hesitated.

He seemed to sense her wavering thoughts and stepped even closer. Dulcie leaned away. He was invading her personal space. Old fears swept over her and her knees went weak.

What seemed like an earnest appeal seconds ago now seemed like a demand. Were her old fears taking over? Was she imagining the change?

"Come on, Dulcie. Just a few minutes of your time. I promise, I won't stay long. I'll tell you all about my project."

The undertones in his voice made her feel like she didn't want to know about his project. And still he crowded her. He was so close her back was up against her door with no room to move.

"Come on, Dulcie." His voice was low, insistent. "Let's go inside and talk." He reached for her keys. Dulcie stood frozen, her gaze focused on his hand, only inches from her keys.

Her phone buzzed.

Joey stared at it as if it were a writhing snake. His pleasant features turned to frowning anger.

Before he could speak, Dulcie tapped the phone symbol on the screen with her thumb. "Hello."

Austin's voice rang over the line. "I'm so glad I caught you. Where are you?"

Dulcie was so relieved to hear his voice, she sagged against the door. "Outside my apartment, talking to Joey." She gave Joey a tremulous shrug. He smiled but it was more of a grimace, and he stepped back out of her space.

There was a conspicuous silence on the other end of the phone.

"Don't say my name, Dulcie." Austin's hastily spoken words froze her again.

"Okay. Why?" She looked at the man standing across from her.

"Listen carefully. Don't talk. Just listen. Joey won't do anything while you have someone on the phone. Tell him this is an important call. You have a family emergency. Tell him you have to go inside. You might even have to leave town. But whatever you do, don't hang up. Keep me on the line. Got it?"

Dulcie took a slow breath. "Yes, yes. I think so. Hang on."

She licked her lips. "I'm sorry, Joey. I have a family emergency. You must excuse me."

His features tightened. "I'm sorry to hear that." His sympathetic words didn't match the tight, cold frustration in his face. "Is there anything I can do? Let me help."

He stepped back into her personal space. Loomed over her. Images flashed through her mind, her father standing over her mother, his fists clenched, his face a mask of fury. Her mother's soft cries echoed in her ears. Time stood still. Her muscles froze.

The man in front of her seemed to sense her inability to move. A small smirk flashed over his lips and a look came into his eyes… A look she knew well. It telegraphed his sense of victory, his knowledge that he had power over her. He had won…and still she couldn't move.

Then Austin's words came over the phone. "Dulcie, are you there?"

His voice, strong, capable, certain. Warm blood coursed through veins. Fear-frozen muscles thawed. Numb fingers twitched. She clenched them around the keys in her hands.

"Dulcie, answer me!"

She took a deep, gasping breath. "Yes. Yes, I'm here. Thank you for your concern. I'm just…a little shocked."

That look she knew so well, that hateful, power-filled certainty, faded from Joey's features. She licked dry lips and addressed him. "There's nothing you can do, Joey. I have to go now."

"Good girl. Keep talking." Austin's voice…confident, protecting her over the phone. He gave her strength. Nodding goodbye, she turned her back on Joey.

Her spine tingled. She could almost feel his gaze shooting daggers into it. For one long, heart-pounding minute she was afraid he wouldn't let her leave, might grasp her shoulders and pull her back. Because of Austin on the phone, listening, guarding, Joey dared not touch her. She fumbled the keys and almost dropped them before fitting the right one into the lock and opening the door. She shut it quickly then slammed the dead bolt into place.

FOUR

Austin flipped on the lights atop his vehicle and sped down the road. Then he called McGuire and told him what had happened.

"Do you want me to send someone over to Dulcie's place?" McGuire asked.

"No. She's safe inside her apartment, but get a hold of Delacroix's license plate for me. We may want to bring someone in to follow him. I want to know who his contacts are."

"Agreed. I'll look into it and see who I can put on it."

Just as Austin pulled into Dulcie's apartment complex, McGuire got back to him with the license plate number and a description of Delacroix's car as well as the name of the deputy he was thinking of bringing into the investigation. Austin approved his choice.

"He's a good man. Hold on a second." He searched the parking lot but Delacroix's vehicle was gone. "He's not here. At least, his car isn't here. I'm going to get Dulcie out of here before he shows up again."

"Good idea. I'll have Bolton there tomorrow morning."

Austin signed off, parked and hurried up to Dulcie's

apartment. He knocked very quietly on her door. A moment or two later, it swung open. Dulcie stayed hidden behind it. As soon as she closed and bolted the door behind him, she threw herself against him.

For one stunned moment, Austin stood with arms outspread. The woman who shied away from him every time he got near had her arms wrapped so securely around his waist he could hardly breathe. He held his arms wide…not sure if he should hug her back or not. Would she appreciate the gesture or feel trapped? He wasn't sure…but it felt good to have her close.

Wet tears soaked the top of his shirt above his bulletproof vest. The soft scent of spring drifted up to him and those wild, untamed curls tickled his cheek. He couldn't help himself. His arms wrapped around her.

"It's all right, Dulcie. I'm here now and he's gone."

She nodded, still clinging to him. "It was such a close call."

Stepping back, she wiped at her cheeks. When most women cried, their noses turned red and their lips and eyes puffed. Dulcie's did too, but on her, those changes softened her features, slightly blurred her bold eyebrows and full lips. Made her look soft and in need of another hug. He almost pulled her back into his arms before he caught himself.

"You're safe now." He sounded gruffer than he intended. But it worked. She straightened and met his gaze.

"You don't understand. He made me feel like I was ten years old again. I froze. Completely froze. I couldn't push him away, couldn't defend myself. I just stood there.

If you hadn't spoken to me…he would have taken my keys right out of my hand…and I would have let him."

She shook her head and stepped away…taking that soft summer scent with her. Austin missed it the minute she moved.

He swallowed and tried to get his thoughts back on track. She was igniting his protective instincts…the ones that always got him in trouble. He needed to pack those responses in a case with steel bands around it.

"He caught you off guard. That's all. You thought he was a friend and he wasn't."

"You're being kind, but any other woman…any normal woman would have at least tried to keep the keys away from him. I just stood there."

Austin didn't know what to say to that. Abey probably would have delivered a flat-palmed punch to his nose…a self-defense move she'd learned in a class she'd brought to the reservation. But Abey wasn't like most women and nothing like Dulcie. He needed to remember that fact.

"All I know is his car is gone. We need to get you out of here before he comes back."

She gestured to a slightly larger than carry-on-sized suitcase. "I'm all packed."

"That's it? Everything is in there?"

She sent him a tremulous smile. "I'm not very high-maintenance, in case you didn't notice." Her tone indicated that was another fault, so unlike other "normal" women. But with Dulcie, the high-maintenance habits of other women were wasted. She had a unique beauty all her own…and it was a shame she didn't know it.

But moments ago, he'd vowed to lock thoughts like that away. Clenching his jaw, he gripped the handle of the suitcase. "Do you have all your files?"

"They're in my bag with my computer." She pulled her heavy winter coat off the sofa. Beneath it was a large satchel bulging with the files. Hitching it on her shoulders, she nodded. "I'm ready."

Austin opened the door a crack and looked up and down the empty hall before stepping out. Dulcie locked the door, and they hurried down the hall and out of the building. Austin checked the parking lot. Delacroix's vehicle was still nowhere to be seen. Nevertheless, once they were in Austin's vehicle, he drove around town for twenty minutes, making right and left turns every half mile to make sure they were not followed. When he was certain no one was behind them, he headed up the mountain to his cabin.

He texted McGuire to let him know he had Dulcie safely in his company and they were driving to his house. McGuire texted back to let him know to park his sheriff's SUV in the garage because he just put out the word that Austin was on vacation and Ms. Parker needed to do the same.

"You need to call in and tell work you had a family emergency and are on your way to California. Hopefully, they'll believe you and it will buy us some time to investigate."

Pulling her coat up tight around her neck, she nodded. "I think they'll believe me. Today one of my coworkers asked me what was wrong. I told her my sister was sick again."

"Again? Does your sister get sick often?"

Dulcie tugged on her coat again. Austin turned up the SUV's heater. "Thanks."

She gave him one of those small, shy smiles, like she was ashamed to ask for basic comforts. "My sister has a lot of health issues. She internalized so much of what we went through…"

Her words trailed off.

"Despite what you're feeling right now, it sounds like you've handled things better."

Her deep sigh filled the vehicle. "Only because my sister stood between me and my dad. She protected me. She took the brunt of his anger." Her voice cracked and she turned her gaze toward the window, away from him. Still, he heard the tears in her tone. "I always felt like the only way to thank her was to be the best I could be, to live a normal, happy life. I don't think I'm doing that very well."

Clouds covered the setting sun and now evening added to the growing gloom in the vehicle. It settled over Austin with a heaviness he recognized all too well.

"You say *normal* a lot. Like it means something. I don't even know what normal means."

That caught her attention. He could feel her gaze on him and this time, he refused to glance her way. He kept his focus on the road ahead.

"But you were married and had a baby on the way. That's normal, isn't it?"

He shook his head. "There was nothing normal about my wife or the life I led with her. She was…amazing. Brave and full of goals and possibilities. It was all I could do to keep up with her." He glanced over. In the twilight of the car, her dark eyes stood out against pale features. "And I never expect to feel that way again."

She met his gaze. A slight frown creased the space between her brows. "I don't think I could live that way… Without hope of something better."

He shrugged. "It depends on what you mean. To me, better is not wishing or wanting something I will never have again. I spent three years of my life wanting her back…wishing things were different. That's a black hole I barely crawled out of. I never want to go back."

He couldn't just leave his thoughts there. He had to probe deeper. "Tell me truthfully. What does *happy* mean to you? What do you need that would give you that happy, normal life you think would be so perfect?"

"I…I don't know."

Shaking his head, he turned back to watch the road. "There you go. Wishing and wanting something you can't even define is a prescription for unhappiness."

He felt her gaze settle on him, as powerful as a touch. He could sense her probing gaze as if she was searching for understanding or answers…and he had neither.

At last she turned away. They were both silent as they sped along the highway, the headlights flashing against the black asphalt and the dense forest around them. He hadn't meant to darken her already complicated life with his own tragedy, but there was something about Dulcie that compelled him to be honest…to open up. Maybe that was her gift, the talent that led her to become a counselor. Whatever it was, he needed to keep his own depressing thoughts to himself.

Gentle snowflakes, the first of the season, began to fall. Soon a white blanket covered the road and the branches of the trees. It brightened the night. Made everything seem clean and white.

"It's coming down pretty hard."

Dulcie nodded. "Yes, and it's beautiful. It's light in the darkness and God's gift to us, to brighten our night."

He glanced at her quickly. She met his gaze defiantly. The little smile tilting her lips was confident, certain and beautiful. Looking at it warmed him, made him want to smile back. He wasn't sure the snow was a gift from God just for them, but he was glad she felt that way.

He turned back to the road. "We'll rest tonight. First thing in the morning, we'll head down to the reservation to see if we can find Doris Begay. I want to talk to her."

"Good. That means my day at work wasn't a complete waste. I looked up her previous address on our records."

"Let's hope she's there. The reservation is too big to try to cover it all."

"How big is it?"

"Over twenty-seven thousand square miles and it stretches across the Four Corners states."

"Wow. I knew it was big but… What if she's not there or we can't find her?"

"I still have a few contacts on the tribal police. We won't come away empty-handed."

He slowed and pulled off the main highway onto a dirt road. "Don't worry. I won't bounce you too much.

I just live far enough from the road to silence the highway traffic noise."

Soon the dirt road opened into a clearing. An A-framed log cabin and a detached garage sat at the back of the clearing. Austin hit the button for the automatic door opener and pulled into the garage. A blue Jeep was parked inside. "I don't use it much, but we'll be driving that tomorrow. My sheriff's vehicle is a little too obvious."

He pulled her suitcase out of the back and led the way to the front porch. He flipped the switch, and light flooded his darkened home. He gestured to the left. "That's the kitchen. It's small but fits my purposes. I don't do much cooking."

"It's not any smaller than my apartment kitchen. Small kitchens work for people who don't spend much time in their places."

"Yeah, I guess that's true. There's a half bath tucked in the corner. The stairs across from us lead to the loft bedroom and the full bath. You'll be sleeping up there."

"Oh no, I can't take your room."

"Yes, you can, and you will. It's an open loft but it offers some privacy and besides, the desk is up there. You'll need it for your research."

She started to protest, but he held up a finger. "I sleep on that sofa more than I sleep on the bed. Trust me—I'll be fine."

She seemed surprised by that and didn't argue. Instead, she looked at the near-empty wall to the right. "Your windows are so high up."

"Yes, but I have quite a view from the loft and those

windows catch a lot of light. They're perfectly placed for the sun's early-morning rays and they warm the house. The guy who built this cabin was environmentally conscious. Speaking of warmth though, I better get the fire going." He gestured to the sofa across from the rock fireplace. "Have a seat. I don't leave the heat on during the day, so first thing I have to do is light a fire."

Showing Dulcie his house made him realize what a utilitarian life he'd been living. There was nothing comfy or homey like Dulcie's place. That realization made him feel like he needed to apologize…again. He seemed to have done that a lot since Dulcie stepped into his life. He didn't understand and what's more, he didn't like it.

He set her case down, stacked the kindling on the hearth and loaded the logs. In moments the fire was blazing. Dulcie sat on the edge of the sofa, shivering, looking like a lost child…who once again shied away every time he stepped near. They were back to that nonsense.

At her apartment she threw her arms around him and now she wouldn't let him step within a foot of her, like he was the threat. It was discomforting, made him unsure of how to respond. He settled for an apology he'd felt the need to give a moment ago.

"I'm sorry it's not as welcoming as your place."

She shook her head and a small, embarrassed smile crossed her lips. "Your home is fine. It's me. I'm just tired. It's been a rough couple of weeks. Actually, a rough two months, ever since Judy disappeared."

Austin couldn't argue with that. Those terrible

months were the reason he'd spent so many nights on the sofa. He'd come home exhausted, eat a frozen pizza and fall asleep in front of the fire only to wake up and do the same the next day.

Frozen pizza. It was the best he had to offer her. "How about some hot chocolate and something to eat? That might help."

She nodded, but her smile was conspicuously absent and…he missed it. Truth be told, he wouldn't mind her in his arms again either. He ached to comfort her in some way. But his arms would only frighten her more.

"Whatever you have is fine with me."

He turned on the oven and heated some water in the microwave for the hot chocolate. When it was done, he handed her the mug. She worked her fingers so they wouldn't touch his. Frustrated, he shook his head.

"I have to feed my chickens. I used to let them roam free but a mountain lion got a few of them so now I keep them in a coop. It won't take me long."

She nodded absently. Austin hurried out. The snow was still falling. His poor chickens were used to his erratic schedule and feedings. He tried to keep their feed bin full in case he didn't make it back in a timely manner. It was near empty so he filled it. When he returned to the now warm cabin, two paper plates and napkins rested on the small wooden table by the loft stairs.

Dulcie came from the kitchen holding the pizza pan with two oven mitts…but she still hadn't removed her coat. "I hope you don't mind me rummaging through your cupboards. I wanted to help."

"No, of course not." He took off his Stetson, hung it

on the rack near the door and washed his hands. Grabbing a knife from the drawer, he sliced the pizza and slid one piece onto her plate. She took two bites, then gripped the mug.

He still felt like apologizing. Was it for his meager accommodations or for her past? He wasn't sure. He just felt like he had to say something. "I'm sorry I don't have anything better."

She shook her head. "The pizza is fine. Really. It's my usual dinner. We have that in common too. I'm just overtired. If it's okay with you, I'm going to head up to bed."

"Sure. Let me show you where the blankets and towels are."

He carried her suitcase upstairs then went back downstairs and finished the pizza. As he cleaned up, he heard the shower running and before he sat down in front of the fire, the light by his bed stand went out. Austin eased back on his couch with a heavy sigh. Dulcie ignited too many contradictory emotions in him. One minute her jumpiness irritated him, the next he wanted to hold her in his arms and protect her from the world. Just the kind of crazy feelings he didn't need to have. She seemed to be as conflicted by him as he was by her. The best thing for both of them was to solve this case and get out of each other's way…and the sooner the better.

Dulcie opened her eyes. Gray light was peeking over the mountain through one of the loft windows. It was just bright enough to see the surrounding forest.

She glanced at the clock. Barely six in the morning. Still, she'd slept almost ten hours. Closing her eyes, she stretched, feeling cozy, comfortable and relaxed. Just having Austin in the house had given her a sense of peace.

She would have stayed in bed longer, but she heard some stirring in the kitchen and soon, the smell of coffee drifted up to her. Her stomach growled. After throwing back the covers, she hopped out of bed and hurried into the bathroom to dress. She hadn't noticed last night but not one of the loft windows had blinds. Given the empty stretches of forest that swept out on each side, with no apparent neighbors, Austin obviously didn't feel the need for window coverings. And he was right not to block the spectacular views. As she made the bed, she marveled at the forest of trees sweeping down the mountain to the valley below. She wondered if on a clear day, you could see all the way to Durango.

Not knowing what they would be doing, she pulled jeans, a long-sleeved knit top and a comfy blue plaid shirt out of her suitcase. As soon as she was dressed, the smell of the coffee lured her to the kitchen where Austin handed her a mug. He looked rested but the dark shadow of a beard graced his cheeks and that wave on his forehead stood straight up. She'd never seen him any other way than clean-shaven and she was surprised by how attractive this slightly rumpled Austin looked.

"Good morning." He nodded but didn't smile. Apparently, an early-morning Austin was not only rumpled but grumpy. That made her smile. There was a boyish quality about him she found incredibly appealing. He looked like a younger, not quite so bitter Austin.

"There's milk in the fridge and sugar in the cabinet if you use it."

"I do. Thanks."

He took another sip. "Since I have nothing for a good breakfast, I thought we might head out early and stop at a place I know in Cortez. It's far enough out of Durango I don't think we'll be seen."

"That sounds good."

"Okay. If you don't mind, I'll grab a shower and we'll take off."

She nodded and he hurried up the stairs two at a time. Dulcie sipped her coffee. The cabin really was a nice place. It just needed a few finishing touches. The wooden ceiling beams were stained a golden color, like the sunshine. She walked into the living room area and ran a hand along the smooth river rock on the fireplace. Still warm from the blazing fire, it emanated a soft heat. She settled on the hearth and imagined what she might do to add some color to this fantastic open area.

Maybe a painting on the wall beneath the high windows…no…one of the beautiful natural handwoven Navajo blankets she'd seen in the stores downtown. A lovely two-handled Navajo horsehair vase, a ceramic in white with black cracks etched on the surface. Thick strands of real horsehair were fired in the pottery and burned away creating the black etchings. Dulcie had seen an example of the craft at the same Native American store where she saw the woven blankets and loved the unique black markings of the pottery immediately.

A large piece would look perfect on the dark rock of the hearth.

She sat content, decorating Austin's empty house in her mind, until he came down the stairs, shaved and with his stubborn little cowlick combed into place.

She smiled. "Your home is amazing. You were right about these windows. They're spectacular."

"I didn't think you were so convinced last night."

"Forget about last night. I was sleep deprived." She really felt like a different person this morning, stronger, brighter, ready to solve the mystery ahead of them. She was sure she owed it to Austin and the confidence his presence gave her. "I had the best night of sleep I've had in months. Thank you."

Her heartfelt words seemed to move him. His crooked smile was genuine. "Well then, let me feed you before you start to feel food-deprived. It'll take me a few minutes to warm up the Jeep. I'll pick you up on the porch." He slid into his hat and coat. Tossing her the keys to the door, he stepped out. The brisk cold air swept into the room, making her thankful he'd volunteered to warm up his vehicle.

She ran upstairs and grabbed a knitted scarf from her suitcase. By that time, she could hear the idling engine just outside the door. After slipping on her jacket, she hitched her purse over her shoulder and locked the door behind her. Austin pulled his shiny blue Jeep close to the rock-lined walkway. The storm had brought two or three inches of snow that lay on the ground like a pristine blanket. It seemed as if her entire world had been washed clean. Austin's golden home full of sunshine. The sparkling snowy perfection around them and the handsome man smiling at her from the driver's seat brought her a joy she hadn't experienced in a long time… Maybe ever. It was hard for her to remember that men were chasing her, determined to do her harm. As if to preserve the perfect moments of the morning, she stayed in Austin's steps on the path, so she wouldn't disturb this soft winter wonderland tucked deep in the forest. Just before she climbed into the Jeep, she glimpsed a small wooden building with chicken wire surrounding it.

Austin took the keys and tucked them into the console. Then he headed down the snow-covered road. It seemed a shame to disrupt the beautiful white covering on the dirt road. Soon they came to the highway. Many cars had already passed over it. The snow had melted and the black asphalt slashed across the white scene with muddy slush on each side. Her winter wonderland was disappearing with every mile they traveled. But one question, one thought lingered.

She couldn't contain it and blurted it out. "Why chickens?"

He turned to her, with a half smile and a half frown. "What about chickens?"

"I mean, why did you choose chickens? Not a usual pet like a dog or a cat."

"Oh, my counselor advised me to find something to care for."

"You went to counseling?"

"I met with my pastor for over a year, trying to forgive myself."

His words gave Dulcie pause. "Why did you need forgiveness?"

He was silent for such a long time, Dulcie thought she'd gone too far, stepped over a boundary he wasn't willing to cross. She bit her lips, sorry that she'd pushed for answers he didn't want to discuss. She turned away.

Then he surprised her with words spoken in a low tone. "I was a sheriff's detective out of Gallup, New Mexico. I knew the dangerous, empty stretch of reservation road Abey traveled over that night, knew the statistics by heart. I should have stopped her from driving home. I...failed to protect... The one thing I took an oath to do when I signed on to become a sheriff. All I ever wanted was to protect people, to help...and yet I couldn't help the most important person in my life."

Dulcie wanted to protest, to tell him he wasn't responsible. She felt the need to reach out and reassure him even though all of her counseling training told her she needed to let him speak. It was all she could do to keep silent. What was it about this man that made her want to act against all she knew? Somehow, he reached deep inside her, passed all her trained barriers to her basic instincts. She didn't know if that was bad or good. She only knew she didn't want him to stop.

"The department counselors finally suggested a transfer. So I applied for the La Plata County Sheriff's Department and made the move, relocated to Durango. I invested in my cabin in the mountains above town, bought a horse, two cows, and let chickens roam over my property. The pine trees and the green were so different from the flat dusty mesas of New Mexico, it changed things. Maybe changed me."

He glanced her way and then back to the road. "At any rate, it didn't seem fair to pick an animal that needed companionship when I'm gone so much of the time. It wouldn't be right to leave a dog home alone most of the day."

It made sense and was fair. But she had the feeling there was more to his thoughts. She wasn't surprised when he continued.

"And besides… I didn't want something I would become too attached to. I couldn't stand losing something else."

His words doused her lovely morning in cold. It was the saddest thing in the world to know that he had that beautiful place in the forest full of sunshine and peace and couldn't enjoy even a small part of it. It seemed so wrong for the caring man she sensed beneath his walled exterior.

She studied him. "Did it work? Did you stay unattached?"

He almost nodded, then a slow, wry smile slipped over his features and a small chuckle escaped. "Are you kidding? Did you see my chicken coop? As soon as I found out some of my chickens were missing and I saw the mountain lion tracks, I went straight to the lumberyard and bought enough wood to build the Taj Mahal of chicken coops. My birds live like kings."

He gave her another quick glance, filled with humor, and she smiled back. Some morning sunshine spilled into her heart. There was more she wanted to say but she left it at that. They both needed that morning sunshine right now.

They traveled down the mountain and through Durango, leaving the forests and the snow behind. They passed the entrance to Mesa Verde National Park, the park that preserved the largest collection of Ancestral Puebloan, formerly known as Anasazi, dwellings in the country. She'd heard all about the park and its cliff dwellings, but she'd never visited. She could easily have made a day trip but somehow, never found the time. That thought made her sad. She loved her work, loved helping the women. Why did she suddenly regret her choices?

Just a few more miles down the road, the snow disappeared. Only a few banks of mud and slush graced the sides of the streets in the small town of Cortez, just fifty minutes away from Durango.

They stopped at a small roadside café and ate a quick breakfast but were back on the road soon. They left the foothills behind and dipped into the open flatlands that led to northern New Mexico. The change of environment came so quickly, Dulcie was in awe. A panorama opened up for her. She could see for hundreds and hundreds of miles. Mountains dotted the vast open area, popping up out of seeming emptiness. To her right was a massive, flat-topped mesa. The sun had not come out in full force, so everything was tinged with soft purples that blended into the dark shadows.

"I've seen numerous paintings of the area, but I never understood why the painters used so many purple and lavender colors. Now I do. It's a true reflection of the land. It's beautiful," she murmured.

Austin nodded. "Yes, it is. We're heading into New Mexico. At sunset, those purple mountains will turn mauve then gray. It looks like a vast empty desert but hidden in all those purple shadows are canyons and wonders. There's a reason New Mexico is nicknamed the Land of Enchantment."

The tone of his voice gave her pause. "You love this land, don't you?"

He studied the view ahead of him. "It's my home, where I grew up. It's a part of me. But it can be a harsh place…unforgiving. I'm not sure I can say I love it anymore."

He pointed to a road up ahead. "That leads to the Four Corners marker where New Mexico, Utah, Colorado and Arizona meet in one spot. You can stand on the marker and be in all four states at one time. The spot is on tribal lands. There's some concessions and a few refreshment stands. Not much to see besides the marker. But you can take a picture with both feet in all four states."

He gave her a small smile that made her wish they could stop right now and take that picture. Not for the first time Dulcie wondered about the effect Austin Turner was having on her.

They traveled for over an hour with Austin pointing out interesting spots and different mesas. At long last they turned off the highway onto a dirt road. They drove for almost thirty minutes on the rough, bumpy, pothole-marked trail.

"I can't believe anyone lives out here. There's nothing. Just a few telephone poles and electric wires."

"Some places don't even have those. The traditional Navajo reject modern conveniences. They stick to the old ways. Plus, the government broke the land into allotments and gave each family a place. In those days they needed lots of land to graze their sheep, so they appreciated the distances between. Things are different now, but they still love their land and the open spaces."

Dulcie allowed her gaze to follow the power lines to where they crested over a hill and dipped down out of view. Sure enough, as the vehicle came to the top of the hill, they looked down on a trailer with several wooden outbuildings and a pen with a few goats. A woman stood in the pen with the animals, pulling apart a bale of hay. As they drove closer, Dulcie recognized Doris Begay. As soon as they were near enough for her to identify them, her body language changed. She shook her head and sent them a scowl meant to keep them at bay.

"Looks like we're not very welcome." Dulcie frowned.

"That's putting it mildly."

Taking a deep breath, Dulcie climbed out of the truck and walked with determination toward the woman. Doris was dressed in jeans and a faded plaid shirt. Her long hair was tied back in a ponytail with wisps of hay caught in it. She turned back to her work so that when Dulcie got close, she had to speak to get her attention. "Hello, Doris."

The woman turned sharply. "Why are you here? Judy's dead and Matt's in jail. What else do you want from me?"

Dulcie halted in her footsteps, shocked by her bitter hostility. She looked at Austin and he continued forward, not backing away from the woman's obvious anger.

"Yes, Matt is in jail. But we think we might have the wrong man."

She shook her head. "He killed my girl. I know it. You need to keep him locked up for the rest of his life."

Austin nodded. "You're so sure he did it, Doris?"

She nodded vigorously. "He did it."

Doris glared at Austin, daring him to deny it.

Austin ducked his head. "I think you're right. Matt killed your girl, but was he alone? Did someone help him?"

The rage fled and her features washed cold and white. The belligerence bled out and she shook her head. "I don't know nothin' about that. Nothin'."

She was lying—Dulcie knew it and so did Austin. He pressed her for more info. "Who was Matt hanging out with before Judy disappeared?"

The woman shook her head. "He didn't need no drinkin' buddies. He did that all by hisself."

"All right, where did he do his drinking?"

She shook her head. "I told you. I don't know nothin'. Now go away and leave me alone." Spinning, she headed toward the house, too angry to say more.

Austin shook his head in frustration. Dulcie couldn't let her get away without more answers.

"What about Susan, Doris? Where can we find her?"

Doris halted in her footsteps. After a long pause, she looked back over her shoulder. "That one is her grandmother's problem. Ask Bea Yazzie."

"Where can we find her?"

She hesitated a moment longer. "At Tséyi. Her hogan is near the White House Trail." With that, Doris Begay marched to the front door of the trailer and slammed the door shut behind her. Austin nudged his head toward the truck. They both headed toward it.

As soon as they slid inside Dulcie said, "Is that it? You're a sheriff. Are you just going to let her shut you out like that?"

"I told you. I have no authority on the reservation."

Sagging, she leaned back on the seat. "I'd forgotten. So, what is Tséyi? Do you have any idea?"

He nodded. "It's Canyon de Chelly, one of the Navajos' sacred places. It's close." He started the engine. "Did you notice she didn't use Susan's name?"

Dulcie caught her breath. "She called her *that one*. Do you think she believes Susan is one of the Missing Ones?"

Austin nodded. "Maybe. One thing is certain—Doris Begay knows a lot more than she's willing to tell us. We're going to need more help."

"What kind of help?"

"I know someone on the tribal police force. I'll call him. But first we'll pay a visit to Susan's grandmother."

He jammed the Jeep into Reverse and backed up. As he turned the truck around, Dulcie's side of the vehicle swerved close to the front of the trailer. Just inside a small window beside the door, she glimpsed Doris peeking out from behind a white curtain and she had an old-fashioned phone held up to her ear. As soon as she saw Dulcie, she jerked her hand away and the curtain fell back into place.

"She's talking to someone on the phone, Austin. I thought you said living out here she wouldn't have any modern conveniences. Do you think she's calling Susan's grandmother to tell her we're coming?"

Austin's features tightened into a grim frown. "Not if Bea Yazzie lives in the canyon. There's no electricity there."

"Then who is she in such a hurry to talk to?"

"That's the million-dollar question, isn't it? Fortunately for us, anyone we need to worry about is in Durango, three hours away. We'll have time to talk to Susan's grandmother and get out of there before they can reach us." He slammed the gearshift into forward motion and kicked a dusty cloud up behind them.

FIVE

As he drove to the highway Austin's mind traced over the time it would take them to get to Canyon de Chelly and back again. They were less than an hour away. Half an hour to trek down the trail and a half hour back up. They might cut it close, but they could make it out of the canyon before the people Doris Begay had called could arrive. One thing about the reservation—it was spread out.

Doris's actions seemed clear to him. She was convinced that Matt Kutchner had killed her daughter and thought he should stay in jail. But she was afraid of the men he'd been hanging around. Too afraid to even name them. She'd come back to the reservation to hide, and now she was willing to buy her safety by reporting their visit to the men she feared. Austin was almost sure that's who she called. Now he and Dulcie had limited time to get in and out before anyone could respond to Doris's call.

But they had to locate Susan Yazzie. Right now, their whole investigation hinged on finding a clue to her whereabouts. If they didn't find that new direction, their trip today was a waste of time…time that was running out. Austin's internal clock was ticking away. Things were coming to a head. He could feel it.

"Tell me about Canyon de Chelly."

Dulcie's question pulled him out of his thoughts. It took him a minute to change gears. "Well, let's see. It's one of the longest continually inhabited places in America. The Navajo have been there since before the Spanish came and some ruins of the Ancestral Puebloans are preserved there too."

"So people have lived in Canyon de Chelly for over a thousand years?"

"Yes, the Ancestral Puebloans lived there for generations before the Navajo people. In fact, Anasazi, the name we used to use to label the Ancestral Puebloans, came from the Spanish. They used the Navajo word for ancient enemies. It doesn't properly describe the people who lived in those dwellings so we stopped using it."

"I thought the only cliff dwellings were at Mesa Verde."

"No, they're dotted all over the Four Corners area. In fact, we'll see some in the canyon. Severe drought and difficult times forced the people of the Chaco culture out of the flatlands into the mountains where there was more water. They built their homes in crevices and clefts for protection using wood and plaster. Some of them look like modern-day apartments with multiple stories. They accessed the top floors by going through rooftop doors and ladders on each level. In some places the only access to the dwellings was by hand- and foot-holds."

"Navajo still live in the canyon?"

"Some stay there year round. But most just live there in the summer when it's warm then leave during the winter. Some traditional folks have hogans, round houses made of logs with mud roofs and a door facing the east. A stream runs right down the middle of the canyon so there's water for their sheep and crops. Navajo sheep are still important to the people. They say their wool is the best for weaving. Many families make their living from weaving rugs and blankets. Abey's grandmother was a weaver."

His voice dropped off as thoughts of his wife flooded his mind. He'd talked about Abey more today than in the past year. Dulcie seemed to do that to him, ignite thoughts he'd tried to suppress. He wasn't sure he liked the feelings those thoughts uncovered.

"Abey…it's lovely. What does it mean?"

"Leaf. It means leaf. Her grandmother wove a blanket for us using wool from her own sheep and natural dyes from plants. The pattern she used is called a storm design, geometric shapes all in earth tones, but she put green leaves in places. It's a true piece of art."

"Where is it?"

"Packed away. I haven't brought it out since I moved."

Dulcie shook her head. "I'm sorry to hear that. It sounds like a beautiful tribute to Abey and her culture. You could hang it on that empty wall in your living room. It would probably look spectacular."

His jaw tightened. She did it again, challenged all the protective barriers he'd put in place, and now he was certain he didn't like it. "It would be a constant reminder."

She nodded. "Yes, but it would be the right kind, a reminder of the good things in her life, not the tragedy of her death."

Austin sent her a sharp glance. "That's strange advice coming from a woman who still suffers panic attacks and freezes every time she gets a reminder of her own past."

The words were out before he could stop them, and he instantly regretted them. Dulcie's features faded and she looked away. But her hurt response only lasted a moment. She turned back to him. The color was gone from her cheeks, but her lips were set in a firm line.

"Who better to give you that kind of advice than someone who constantly fights to keep the fear at bay?"

His shoulders sagged. "You're right. I'm sorry. I was out of line. I just… I don't talk about Abey."

Her expression was achingly honest. "I understand, Austin. I truly do. I couldn't talk about my childhood for years. It was too horrible. But finally, I started remembering some good times. And that's how I fought the bad. I try to remember the wonderful blessings the Lord sent to comfort me through the bad times. Sometimes I struggle to find the good things, but it's worked… until now."

He was certain she was referring to her recent bout of dangerously debilitating fear when faced by Delacroix. He wouldn't add more fuel to the fire of her disappointment. Right now, she needed encouragement more than truth…especially after his unkind comment a moment ago. "Give yourself a break. It's not every day a person's life is threatened. It's not surprising you've suffered a setback."

She sighed. "Maybe, and maybe the Lord has a new lesson for me."

Austin smiled in spite of his conflicted emotions. "You're finding the good in your bad situation, right?"

She laughed, a sweet little sound he hadn't heard come out of her. She had laughed little, if at all, since they'd met. "I guess. See? It's a good habit to form."

He tilted his head. "It's not a habit I need. Blessings don't come my way."

"Or…you've forgotten how to recognize them when they do."

He slowed the Jeep as they came into Chinle, the town leading to the canyon.

"I think we need to grab some lunch. There's a drive-through up ahead. Will that work for you?"

"Sure."

He pulled in and ordered some burgers and fries. Keeping busy gave him an excuse not to talk. He handed her the bag and pulled onto the road. Eating also gave him an excuse for not talking, but it didn't shut down his mind from churning.

Was she right? Had he forgotten how to recognize the Lord's hand moving in his life? He never gave up believing that God was out there…somewhere. He just felt that the Lord had stopped working in his life. He'd clung to his pastor's counsel, attended church most every Sunday and yet…his faith life had been empty. He felt like God had abandoned him the night Abey died.

Is that how he really felt…? Abandoned? Had he just been going through the motions of his faith?

He couldn't remember a single instance where he'd felt loved by God…even *felt* the Lord's presence. Dulcie was wrong. He hadn't forgotten how to see God. He had been abandoned. One dark night, on a lonely stretch of highway, God turned His back on Austin Turner.

"Doris alerted the ring about our visit, didn't she?" Dulcie's question broke into his thoughts. Her tone was so low, he almost couldn't hear her.

In spite of her determination, it seemed she couldn't keep her concerns completely under control. His mind searched for the right way to answer, one that wouldn't trigger her into a frozen state. "She didn't come home to find her 'roots.' We still don't know *who* she's hiding from, but she's definitely hiding."

"It doesn't make sense. Why would she call them? How could she help the men who murdered her daughter?"

"She blames her husband for her daughter's death, and since he's in jail for that crime, I don't think she sees it as helping them. Besides, she's afraid to end up like her daughter. She'll give those men what they want to protect herself, even if what they want is us."

Dulcie slowly nodded. "I understand that. My note said I'd become a Missing One too. It frightened me into unexpected actions."

Austin tried to reassure her. "Look, the reservation is a big place and the canyon has a lot of visitors. People will surround us and it's almost a three-hour drive from

Durango. By the time any of our suspects can reach the canyon, we'll be long gone."

His phone rang. McGuire's name flashed on the screen. He punched the button on his console to answer. "Hello."

McGuire's gruff voice rang over the air. "Glad I caught you. I've got some bad news. The municipal police got a call last night to investigate a break-in. Someone trashed Ms. Parker's apartment."

Cold washed over Austin. He looked at Dulcie. Concern was reflected in her gaze.

He gripped the steering wheel. "They were looking to snatch her and destroy her research."

"That was my thought."

"Who called in the report?"

"The couple in the apartment below Ms. Parker heard banging, things falling and reported it. By the time the officers got there, the intruders were gone. I've asked for a complete report from the munis."

"I'll be surprised if Officer Shaw doesn't try to suppress the info."

"Officer Shaw hasn't reported for duty in two days. According to one of his fellow officers he's missing."

"A missing police officer? That didn't trigger an all-out search?"

"It did. It was good to have the munis on board and… they found some suspicious activity on Shaw's computer."

"I'm surprised he didn't wipe it clean before he left."

"Maybe he didn't know he was leaving."

Austin's churning thoughts came to an abrupt halt.

If Shaw was missing… "What about Delacroix? Did the officers question him?"

"They tried but there was no answer at his apartment. A resident said they saw him leaving the day before around three p.m. This morning his car was found at the bottom of a cliff on Wolf Creek Pass. There were skid marks and two sets of tire tracks."

Austin knew exactly what that meant. Delacroix was dead…probably at the hands of his partners in crime. He glanced at Dulcie and tried to frame his words in a way that wouldn't terrify her.

"Sounds like they're eliminating all their weak links."

"And all our leads."

Austin took a slow breath. All their leads except Dulcie. His efforts to reframe his words failed. She'd connected the dots and was afraid.

"Did they find anything in Dulcie's apartment that might lead us to the perpetrators?"

"No prints, nothing tremendously helpful except for one thing. It wasn't a break-in. Someone picked the lock, a professional job. I had Bolton create a list of all the local criminals with that skill."

McGuire read the names but Austin knew one that would be on there before his lieutenant even said it. Austin was very familiar with Walter Benally and his career of crime. The man's involvement sent another spike of worry through Austin.

He glanced at Dulcie, fearful that his concern might show. She'd clamped her lips tight with tension and turned her gaze away.

"Things are getting dangerous, Austin. I want you and Ms. Parker back as soon as possible."

Austin hesitated. "We're twenty minutes out from Bea Yazzie's place. So far Susan Yazzie is our only lead. We need to find her."

McGuire was silent for a lengthy pause. "All right, but you need to make Ms. Parker aware. It should be her choice. If she decides to go on, I want you to stay in touch."

"We won't have reception in the bottom of the canyon but I'll do my best."

Austin clicked off. The gang was sending their members into hiding or maybe even killing them off. They were risking exposure to cover their tracks and eliminate any evidence. Those actions increased Dulcie's danger incrementally…not to mention the fact that if Benally was involved, there was a good chance Johnny Whitehorse was involved too. Benally worked for Whitehorse, who owned The Round Up bar located just off the reservation. The men after Dulcie could be closer than he thought and he'd just talked McGuire into letting them go farther away from safety. Was he wrong? Was he taking too big a risk, expecting too much from Dulcie…and maybe even himself?

He glanced her way again…once…twice. She wouldn't meet the unspoken question in his gaze and her lips were pinched in a tight line.

"You heard about Delacroix?"

She nodded, a tight dip of her head. "But I'm not sure I understand the significance of two sets of tire tracks."

Austin inhaled. "The skid marks mean Delacroix

tried to brake and stop his descent. The other set of tires means another vehicle was behind him, pushing him off."

She jerked. "You think his partners in the ring pushed him off the road?"

"That looks like a possibility, yes."

Shock washed over her features. "He was one of them…he tried to kidnap me…for them. If they'll do that to one of their own…" The obvious conclusion hung in the air between them.

"We don't know exactly what turned them against him, Dulcie. He might have done something wrong. Maybe he felt guilty about his treatment of you and wanted to speak out. McGuire has put in a request for a search warrant for Delacroix's apartment. Perhaps we'll find an answer there."

She looked ahead, her churning emotions clearly written on her face. Then her features froze. "I was his project," she murmured.

Austin turned to her. "What do you mean?"

"When we were standing outside my door, Joey said he was about to finish a long-term project. I was his project, Austin. He'd been spying on me, watching me the entire time I lived there. When I discovered the ring, he was about to turn me over, but I escaped. He failed and now he's dead."

Austin nodded slowly. "It makes sense. He tried to run so they followed him." Reaching across the space, he grasped her hand. "Dulcie, they're eliminating all their loose ends and you are a loose end. They'll be even more focused on catching you now."

She closed her eyes and took deep breaths. Austin linked their fingers and squeezed.

"McGuire gave us permission to go on but like he said, the decision is up to you. We can go to Bea Yazzie's hogan or we can turn around and head back to safety right now."

He gripped her hand tightly. His touch seemed to give her strength.

"No," she murmured, struggling to find her voice. "We have to go on. Susan is a loose end too. She's somewhere out there, hiding or running or maybe in their grasp. We have to find her."

Relief swept through Austin. He released her and gave her a one-sided smile.

"That's my girl."

She rubbed her hands up and down her arms as if a sudden chill had entered the Jeep cab. He was happy she agreed to go on but concern assailed him. If her fears finally overcame her, he'd have to leave her in the vehicle while he hiked down the two-mile trail by himself.

Wait…could Dulcie even hike down the trail? Right now she looked about as fragile as a porcelain doll. Maybe she wasn't up to that kind of strenuous activity. How could he have been so stupid as to not consider that possibility? If she wasn't up to it, he'd have to reformulate his plans.

"Hey, I forgot one little detail. The trail is two miles down and back. Are you up to that kind of walk?"

Dulcie took a deep breath, looked at him beneath lowered brows and sent him a mysterious, sort of flirty smile that knocked his socks off. Where did that come from?

She pushed her long russet-colored locks over one shoulder and said, "I can probably beat you down and back up."

Austin chuckled. He couldn't help himself. What had suddenly made her so confident?

"Was that a challenge?" He couldn't keep the teasing out of his tone and he didn't try. He liked this slightly sassy, flirty Dulcie.

She flashed a brilliant, hundred-watt smile that literally took his breath away. This…this was the wild, untamed woman hiding beneath the waiflike little girl. Here was the real Dulcie, the woman she kept tamped down with tight hairstyles and ugly, baggy clothes. The real woman afraid to come out from behind the frightened child. Did she know how her sun-burnished curls and brilliant smile could light up a day…his day?

"I think it *was* a challenge. Are you up to it, Deputy Turner?"

His chuckle was out before he could stop it. How did she do this…keep him off-balance and pull emotions out of him…emotions he hadn't felt in a long time?

He wasn't sure. He only knew that for a change, he was enjoying himself. "Just so you know, in my division, I ran the fastest mile in our POST…peace officers standards test."

Her eyebrows perked up and she tilted her head back and forth in another sassy movement. "Was it faster than nine minutes? Because that's my best."

"Whoa, are you serious? That's pretty good for a woman of your stature."

A sad smile wavered over her lips. "What you really mean is a scaredy-cat like me."

Not giving him time to answer, she said, "You shouldn't be surprised. Heavy-duty exercise means good endorphins to fight depression. I've been a runner since my first therapist recommended it when I was fifteen. I admit most of my running these days is on the treadmill in my apartment complex's gym. But I do love hiking too. If I'd known about Canyon de Chelly's trail, I would have tried to make it here before now."

Austin eyed her askance. "Do you really think the trail could have lured you away from your needy women?"

She turned to him, her expression wide open and so vulnerable it was almost painful to see. "No," she said. "Probably not the trail by itself."

Austin's breath hitched. Was she hinting that he might coax her out for a hike? All his teasing fled and he focused his gaze on the road. What was he doing?

Encouraging a broken woman to open up to a man who had nothing to give was wrong, just wrong. He needed to stop this right now. He couldn't think of anything to say, a way to apologize or explain, so he just kept silent. Fortunately, they'd arrived at the parking lot of the trailhead.

He pulled into a parking space among the others. Many visitors stood near the ledge overlooking the canyon. Dulcie walked toward the lookout as Austin pulled two bottles of water from the box he kept in the back of his Jeep and tucked them in his jacket pockets. Living and working in such isolated places, he'd learned to keep water and supplies on hand.

A cool breeze swept up from the bottom of the canyon and lifted the ends of Dulcie's burnished curls. A slight smile wavered over her coral lips as she stared at the sight on the sandstone cliff across from them. Dark pigment washed down from the canyon rim above and covered parts of the cliff, giving it the shiny gleam called desert varnish. Six hundred feet below the rim, tucked in a narrow, horizontal slice in the bluff were the ruins. Time-washed plaster turned white covered some towers and upper buildings and had earned the site its Navajo name, Kinii' ni gai… White House. Below the cliff rooms, on the canyon floor, were more abodes.

"Archaeologists say the towers were once tall enough to reach the top level. That's how the builders got to the upper rooms. That's unusual for pueblo ruins. Usually the inhabitants used ladders and hand- and footholds to climb up and down."

"It must have been a difficult way to live, and yet…"

Her gaze travelled up and down the canyon below. A wide sandy wash swept down the middle, dotted with water-loving cottonwoods. Both those trees and the willows along the bank of the *arroyo* had lost most of their leaves. But the empty branches had a regal look. Even with winter nipping at its edges, the canyon still carried a beauty all its own.

"It's unique and amazing," Dulcie said.

Her words sent a spike of pleasure shooting through Austin. He was glad to know she valued the canyon in the same way he did. But it was also one more thing

Austin needed to ignore. If he wasn't careful, Dulcie would break through his protective wall and that was not a good thing. She wouldn't understand that his wall was there for other people's protection. The man behind that wall was empty, drained, living a half life. Dulcie and her innocent ways needed to stay on the other side for her own emotional safety.

"We don't have time for sightseeing. We need to get going on that trail. Dark comes early to the canyon." His words sounded gruffer than he meant, but maybe it was best that way. Dulcie would be safer.

Austin started for the trail, leaving Dulcie standing alone on the edge. She trembled at the full realization of the threat facing her. Her senses, every nerve in her body weakened.

Joey had threatened her, pushed her against the wall intending to trap her so he could hand her over to the violent men of the ring. The feeling of powerlessness he'd ignited inside her washed through her again. She felt trapped, suffocated…powerless…and now…the man who had made her feel helpless was dead…probably murdered by the very men who were his partners.

Austin's words echoed in her mind. *The decision is up to you.*

Up to her. She had choices…options. She was not a trapped little girl, powerless to take action or even move. Her gaze darted to Austin as his tall form took the trail. He seemed full of strength and purpose. She could have kissed him for the courage he gave her. Instead, she took another long, deep breath and followed him.

Dulcie concentrated on moving one foot after the other. She felt awkward and weak at first, but soon, her body found a rhythm. The exercise felt good. Stress and fear poured out of her and into the ground with each pound of her foot on the dusty trail. Soon the path narrowed and they walked along bluffs of sandstone. Large red boulders dotted the sides of the trail and piñon trees and evergreens sent the smell of pine into the air.

Soon, she felt stronger and maybe even peaceful. Yes, men were chasing her. Yes, other women were in danger…and maybe lost forever. Those were realities. But she felt guided, purposeful and she owed it all to the man in the cowboy hat and dusty boots leading the way.

Matching him stride for stride, seeing an outcropping or a bird darting across the sky, she'd turn to see Austin noticing the same thing. They saw things, enjoyed the small delights of nature in the same way. This walk along the trail—being with him—gave her a sense of companionship she'd only known with her mother and sister. It was unique and thrilling. What would it be like to see the Grand Canyon with him, or the red rocks of Sedona? She could think of a myriad of trips she would enjoy sharing with him. He'd called her his girl. If only…

Dulcie almost stumbled over her own feet as surprise washed over. In her life, there'd never really been an "if only" moment with a man. Of course, she'd hoped for moments like this, but with most men, she'd always found herself tensing up, closing in on herself. The second they raised their voices, all her old fears flooded in and any burgeoning relationship would end. She'd had those moments with Austin too, especially in the beginning. But now that she knew him better, those moments came farther and farther apart. So many other things about him gave her peace... The concern he tried to hide for the missing girls. The respect he had for her gave her confidence and she felt herself unfolding like a flowering bloom. It was an unexpected blessing and she thanked the Lord as they hiked down the trail.

They passed through two tunnels carved into the rock and finally came to a flat area. Off the path, tucked around an outcropping of rock, Dulcie glimpsed the edge of a round, wooden structure. A sign along the dirt trail leading to the hogan commanded them to respect the privacy of the occupant.

"This is it." Austin stepped onto the path leading to the home.

Dulcie scooted to catch up with him. "Are you sure? The signs are very clear about not trespassing."

"This is the only hogan on the trail. It has to be the right one."

Around the corner, the outcropping of buff-colored rocks concealed more flat land with small corrals and pens. A Navajo woman crossed from the hogan to a trough with a metal bucket in her hand. A black-and-brown dog trotted by her side. Sheep in the small pen headed for the trough when they saw her coming. Dulcie smiled. The woman's animals knew her and responded, an action Dulcie didn't expect to see from sheep.

The woman wore traditional clothing, a full-length skirt that looked like dark blue velvet. A long-sleeved blouse of the same material. And a silver concha belt was looped around her tiny waist. Her silver hair was tied in a traditional Navajo bun. As they drew closer, Dulcie realized the woman was much older than she'd first thought. Susan's grandmother didn't look strong enough to carry the heavy bucket of water. Her face was long and weathered from days in the sun, but her features wore a serene expression Dulcie would not forget for a long time. There was such peace in that expression. She longed for that kind of peace.

"Ya ta he." Austin called out the greeting.

The woman turned. She was neither startled nor frightened by their presence, but she tilted her head and squinted her eyes, trying to see them clearly.

"Ma'am, my name is Austin Turner and this is Dulcie Parker. I'm a deputy from the La Plata sheriff's department. We'd like to talk to you about your granddaughter."

"So, you have found her?" The woman's voice was low and raspy. It took both Austin and Dulcie a moment to understand her. When they did, they glanced at each other.

"No, ma'am. We weren't sure she was missing."

"She has been gone two months but my nephew was on a long trip. When he came back, I told him to go to the men at that place…that tribal police. They said they would make a report."

Dulcie and Austin shared another glance. If a report was generated, Officer Shaw obviously had done his work and suppressed it. Austin shrugged. "I'm sorry, ma'am. I didn't receive the report, but I'd like to help you find her."

She studied him, then looked past him to Dulcie. Finally, she nodded. "Come. We will have coffee."

Heading toward the hogan, she never looked back.

Dulcie grabbed Austin's arm. "We don't have time for coffee. You said we had to get in and out before someone has a chance to follow us."

"We don't have a choice. It would be disrespectful not to take the offer now that she's made it. If we want the information, then we will drink coffee."

Dulcie followed him but couldn't help but glance back at the trail and up the cliff's face. The path was empty, and that took some of the edginess off her nerves.

A small table with chairs stood just outside the hogan. The woman had already returned from inside with three mugs and an old-fashioned metal coffeepot. Steam poured out of the spout into the cool air. The smell drifted toward Dulcie, roasted and rich and more appealing than she would have imagined. They settled at the table and Bea Yazzie poured.

Austin engaged the older woman by asking if she used the wool of her sheep for weaving. She answered yes, and they chatted for a while about her Navajo sheep and the natural dyes she used for their soft wool.

"I use my grandmother's loom. It's very old. Even older than me." Her dark eyes twinkled and Dulcie found herself warming to the woman. Austin deftly and gently brought the conversation back to her missing granddaughter. Dulcie noted that although she didn't refer to Susan by name, she didn't speak of her as if she was already gone.

But Doris Begay had referred to Susan as a *Missing One*. What did she know that the rest of them didn't?

According to Susan's grandmother she had been missing since the night of Judy's murder. Bea Yazzie had thought her granddaughter was living with a friend, but since she had no cell phone, she had to wait to call Susan until her nephew returned.

"I knew she was in trouble. My granddaughter, she always talks about Doris Begay's man. He is a bad father. I told my granddaughter…both girls, you come live with me in the canyon. Stay away from that bad man. But they wouldn't come. Now look what happened." She shook her head. "Young people today want all the wrong things. Those girls want to look like movie stars. They always worry about makeup and clothes and go to that drinking place to show off."

Across the table, Austin tensed. "What drinking place?"

"That one, just off the reservation. You know, John Whitehorse's place."

"You mean The Round Up?"

She nodded. "That place is no good…no good for no one. Not men, and for sure, not young girls."

Austin asked her a few more questions, about other friends of Susan's he could contact, other places she frequented. But the young woman lived in Durango and only visited occasionally. Her grandmother knew little about her life in the city. Austin seemed eager to leave now, more than anxious. He thanked the woman many times but rose firmly. "It's getting late. We must leave the canyon before dark."

The older woman nodded. She studied his face and

looked deep into his eyes. "Yes, you are the one. You will find my granddaughter."

He gave a shake of his head. "I will do my best. But I can't make any promises."

The old woman nodded once more. "You will find her."

Austin rose and strode toward the trail. Dulcie said goodbye and followed him. He inspired good feelings in all women, not just herself. But that fact didn't seem to please him. He hurried up the trail and Dulcie was hard-pressed to keep up. Almost out of breath she said, "Are you taking my dare seriously? Are we racing up the trail?"

He paused and turned back to her, his features set and hard. "I made a mistake. I was so anxious to get to the truth, I was overconfident. I should have known better...thought it through."

"What do you mean?"

"I should have known Whitehorse is involved. He's got a hand in every crime racket in the Four Corners states." He started up the trail again.

"So? That just gives us someone else to investigate."

"You heard Bea. Whitehorse's place is where vulnerable women go to get noticed. Only it's probably not the kind of notice they're looking for. Whitehorse also has the right men, the kind who can muscle a girl into a truck and transport her."

Dulcie halted. "You're saying you think Whitehorse is the leader of the gang."

Austin kept his gaze on the trail and hurried forward. Dusk was slipping into the canyon very rapidly and the trail was disappearing. Another few moments and the cliff walls would block all light. A chill came with it, settling over them with a gloom that went deeper than a simple setting of the sun.

"I don't know if he's the leader. He has the muscle, but I doubt he has the means to contact a buyer on an open market. That would take someone with a little more national or international exposure."

She hurried to catch up. "Someone like DA Havlicek or Kent Pierce."

"Yeah. Exactly like those two, but which one? And most important of all, how do we prove it? We haven't pulled up one single piece of evidence except Delacroix's fingerprint on your threatening letter and he's already been eliminated."

Out of breath, she halted. "It also doesn't explain why we're running up the canyon wall."

Austin paused long enough to grab her hand and pull her forward. "I told you—I took the wrong chance. I assumed we could beat the people looking for you out of the canyon but I was wrong. Doris Begay is terrified of someone, and now, I'm pretty sure that someone is Johnny Whitehorse. When she made that call, it was probably to him and his place is only an hour away. His men might be on their way or already here."

Dulcie's heart skipped a beat and she stumbled behind him but Austin didn't let up his pace. He marched ahead, climbing so fast Dulcie's legs and lungs burned. They passed through the first near dark tunnel. Then climbed past the piñon pines to the second tunnel where Dulcie pulled her hand loose and stopped. Her lungs were on fire and she needed to stop for a moment to catch her breath.

Austin halted too. In that moment, they heard voices. Two men talking quietly, their footsteps scattering rocks as they made the descent on the other side of the tunnel.

Dulcie stared at Austin, wide-eyed, her heart pounding when they both heard one man say her name. It echoed through the tunnel, muted, but clear enough to understand. They were here for her. Without another word, Austin grabbed her hand again and bolted back down the trail.

SIX

Fool! Idiot! Stupid!

Austin called himself names as he pulled Dulcie down the narrow trail. How could he have been so foolish? He should have known Whitehorse would be involved in an operation this big. When Dulcie saw Doris Begay on the phone in her trailer, he should have escorted Dulcie back to a place of safety. Now she and Susan's grandmother were in danger. Not only did he have to get Dulcie away from the men behind them, but he had to make sure they didn't make a stop at the Yazzie hogan.

Darkness was looming. Shadows made the trail difficult to see. They came to the second tunnel and Austin had to use the light on the cell phone to get them through. It was a beacon for the men above them to follow, but it was better than tripping and falling.

How many voices had he heard? At least two distinct ones but there could be other silent men with them. Could he hold off two or more men on his own? He had his service revolver but no way could he afford bullets flying everywhere. Dulcie could be hurt. Better to get to the canyon floor where they could hide in the myriad of curves and pitch-black crevices of the cliffs. Then they could find another way out of the canyon trail. But first…they had to get past the Yazzie hogan. The last thing he wanted was for the men to harm Susan's grandmother.

They came out of the tunnel and he switched off the light. At this section of the trail, piñon trees covered each side, hiding them from view. Just ahead was the turnoff trail to the hogan. A rocky abutment hid the home but a wide-open space between the trail and rocks was clearly visible from the trail above. He wanted to make sure the men following them saw and knew that they didn't take the path leading to the Yazzie place. He would need to time it carefully so the men could see that he and Dulcie had run down to the canyon floor.

Just as they hit the open space, Austin pushed Dulcie ahead. "Keep going. Don't stop. I'll catch up."

"Why…"

"No questions, Dulcie, just get going!"

She spun and ran to the next turn in the trail, out of his view. Austin scanned the face of the cliff. Two dark figures emerged from the tunnel. Good. Only two men. And their exit out of the tunnel was perfect timing. He could see their excited hand gestures in the gloomy darkness.

They saw him. Suddenly…one man pointed. There was something in his hand. A shot reverberated through the canyon. A bullet pinged off the ground ten feet away from Austin, followed by angry words echoing in the canyon. One man wasn't pleased his partner had fired. Austin didn't wait to see which of the men had the gun. Spinning, he followed Dulcie down the trail.

So, the men were definitely armed. That confirmed his suspicions. He couldn't risk Dulcie getting caught in the crossfire. Nor could he risk getting trapped in a rocky culvert with no way out. He knew there were other trails out of the canyon, but he didn't know where they were and would probably miss them in the dark. Somewhere down the canyon someone might have an ATV or a means of transportation, but they could be miles away and asking for their help would put those people at risk. Chances were most canyon residents had already left for their winter homes. Very few of the families were like Bea Yazzie, who was set in her ways and lived in the canyon all year long. That left only one place they could hide where they would have an exit.

The ancient ruins. Austin hated the thought of possible damage to the ruins but if it meant saving Dulcie, he would do it.

For years, he'd assisted a friend with the yearly inspection of the ruins and had explored them up close. There were two levels, a ground floor and another level resting on a ledge high above the bottom. The ground floor had a tower with multiple levels. It was too damaged to climb, but there were many rooms on the floor level and even a niche deep at the back, beneath the massive bluff. If necessary, he could tuck Dulcie in that crevice and lead the men away. Besides, if the men had to search each small cubby room in the ruins, that would give Dulcie and Austin time to get out and head back up the trail. Hiding in the ruins was their best option.

He came around a corner and almost ran into Dulcie coming back up the path. "I told you not to stop."

"I heard the shot. I thought you might be hurt."

"Everyone for a mile in both directions heard the shot. Let's hope one of them has the means to get help." Grabbing her elbow, he hurried her back down the path.

"Do you think those men would hurt Susan's grandmother?"

"If one of those men is Walter Benally—he would hurt his own grandmother if there was money involved." His words came out in a low tone. They reached another bend in the trail below with a view of the front of the hogan. It was silent and dark, as if no one was there. Even the sheep had moved into the corral beneath the ramshackle covering against the rock wall. "I think Bea is used to taking care of herself. Besides, I made sure they saw me. My guess is they're more intent on getting their hands on you."

At least that's my hope. He glanced one more time at the hogan and sent up a prayer for the old woman's safety…and theirs.

The trail flattened out. Piñon pines gave way to tamarisk and olive trees—non-native, invasive trees taking over the park and most of the Southwest. Right now, Austin was thankful for their coverage. They came to the flat, sandy wash of the riverbed. The snowstorm had blanketed the mountains but had not yet reached the desert, so the wash was dry. Across the streambed, a wire fence surrounded the ruins, blocking them off from trespassers. With a glance at the cloud-filled, moonless sky and the cliff above, Austin led Dulcie from bush to bush, hiding and darting to avoid being seen. At last they made it to the other side. He followed the fence to the rock cliff where it ended with massive wooden posts. Gripping the fence, he climbed over.

Dulcie's harsh whisper echoed beneath the bluff. "We're stopping here?"

"It's our best chance. Come on."

Without another moment's thought, she climbed over, evidence of her trust in him. Too bad she trusted him so much. So far, he hadn't done a very good job of staying ahead of the gang's plans. But wasn't that the story of his life?

He shook off his negative thoughts and led the way to the ruins. "Be careful. Step where I step and don't lean on any walls or supports." He kept his voice low so it didn't echo in the empty chambers. Dulcie didn't speak and he didn't look back to see if she acknowledged his order. Finding his footing took all of his concentration.

There was no way to enter the ruins proper from the left side. They had to cross in front…in plain view from above. Austin could only hope the men following them were focused on the trail. Ducking, he pulled Dulcie across the open space and around the remains of a large kiva—a deep, circular pit. Austin headed between two walls and led her all the way to the back, where a narrow door with a T-shaped frame fed into the dark interior. On the opposite wall, another door led into a warren of rooms that once served the small but bustling community. Other doors led farther and farther back until the ruins dipped beneath the massive cliff wall. Austin didn't want to enter the deeper parts of the ruins if he didn't have to. But if he did, the small doors and rooms were hard to traverse and would slow their pursuers down. Hopefully that would give Dulcie and him time to escape from the other side. At least that was his plan.

Please, God, let this work. Let me do this part right.

At the back of the narrow passage, two wooden beams supported the wall to their right. It was a good place to hide since the shadows there were deep, but he could still see down the narrow opening and across the riverbed.

"Sit down and lean against the supports…but only the supports, not the walls. Rest while you can." Dulcie nodded in response to his whispered words and eased down on ground worn hard and smooth by years and use. Unfortunately, both their raspy breaths echoed in the empty passage.

Austin crouched down beside her. "Take some deep breaths. Let's slow it down."

She nodded. With silent gestures, he motioned for her to follow his deep breaths. She obeyed and several inhalations slowed and silenced their heavy breathing… and just in time.

They heard the low voices of the men standing outside the fence around the ruins.

"I'm telling you. That's the only place they could have gone."

"Nah. They could be hiding behind any of those trees down the wash. We need to keep going."

Austin's worst fear was realized when he recognized the raspy voice of Walter Benally. Bob Carson's mother told Austin her son was running with Benally. Was Carson the other man?

Whoever he was, he was insistent. "I'm telling you, man. They're hiding in those old rooms. Let's go look."

Austin tensed.

"I'm not gonna waste time searching all those rooms when they've probably gone down the trail," came the raspy reply. "Besides. I don't go near the houses of the ancient ones."

Ancient ones. The people of the Navajo Nation often referred to the Ancestral Puebloans as the ancient ones...and they had tremendous respect for their ruins. The man's use of the term confirmed his conviction that Benally was one of the men.

"How far is the next house on the wash?" the other man asked.

Benally sounded irritated. "I don't know. I don't spend no time here if I can help it. The place gives me the creeps. Besides, we don't want anyone to see us. You already caused enough noise with that shot, Carson."

Austin clenched his fist with conviction. He should have paid more attention to Carson's mother when she told him about the connection. He wished he'd followed through and done more. If he had, they wouldn't be here now.

"Sorry. I thought it might scare him into stopping. So what are we gonna do?"

"Let's go down the trail a ways. See if we can't get

to a high spot where we can look down on the floor. We can see most everything from there."

They moved away from the fence and down the trail. Austin listened until he could no longer hear their movement. It was long enough for Dulcie to settle herself from their strenuous run down the trail. She had begun to shiver. Austin pulled the water bottle out of his pocket and cracked the lid. Even that small sound echoed in the cavernous passage. They both tensed. When nothing happened, he handed the bottle to her and she drank. Austin opened the other bottle and took his own sip before carefully and silently creeping toward the opening so he could look down the wash. The men walked along the white edges of the sandy riverbed. Suddenly, they paused and stood for a long while. It appeared they were arguing again. Then one of them spun and stalked back their way. Austin hurried to where Dulcie sat, knees drawn up, head resting on her folded arms. Her whole body shivered.

Lifting the snap on his firearm holster caused her to raise her gaze. Austin knelt low and whispered, "They're coming back our way. If one of them crosses the fence, I will shoot. If I fire, I want you to run to the back. There's a deep crevice in the rock wall. Go as far as you can and hide. I'll try to lead them away."

She started to shake her head, but he held his finger to his lips. The men's muffled voices reached them and Dulcie held whatever protests she'd been about to make. The two men stopped at the same place along the trail and once again, their voices carried over the wash. Austin pressed back as close to the fragile wall as he dared.

He wished he could lean out far enough to get a glimpse of their faces. He wanted visual proof that they were who he thought. If he and Dulcie got out of this canyon safely, he'd be on the radio to McGuire to have them arrested. But if Carson convinced Benally to climb the fence and cross to the ruins, they wouldn't get out of here unscathed. Austin gripped his pistol.

"I still think they're hiding in those ruins." Carson's voice caused Austin to tense and hold his breath. He dared not even remove the safety on his gun in case it clicked loudly in the narrow passage.

"I told you. I'm not going in there!" Benally was adamant. Austin released his breath.

Benally continued, his tone marking his irritation with Carson. "For all we know, they could have hidden in the trees along the trail. We could have easily missed them in the dark."

"Too bad the moon's not out. You really think they got behind us and doubled back to the parking lot?"

After a long silence, Benally said, "I don't know. Let's go back. If his Jeep is still there, we'll wait for them. They have to come up sometime."

"What if they climb out someplace else?"

"We have a better view of the whole canyon from the lookout. We'll see them if they move up or down the wash. Besides, it's miles to the closest help."

Austin heaved a sigh of relief and closed his eyes as the men walked away. He couldn't believe how fortunate they'd been. Only Benally's deep respect for the ancient Puebloans had saved them. Relief swept through him making him sag. He waited a long while before he crept to the opening of the passageway and peeked out. He watched the trail leading up the side of the cliff. Two dark shadows moved across the opening below Bea Yazzie's hogan. The small house was dark and showed no signs of life. He hoped Benally and Carson believed it was empty, but Austin didn't move until he saw them crossing the next clearing above the path to her place. Releasing his breath in a long sigh, he holstered his gun and walked back to Dulcie.

She sat huddled on the ground, shaking from head to toe. She looked so cold and tired and miserable. All he wanted was to pull her in his arms and hold her. But he wasn't sure how that gesture would be received. One minute she appreciated his help. The next she shied away.

He eased down beside her, his back against the support. After a minute of watching her abject misery, he couldn't stand it. Opening the folds of his coat, he pulled her close and tucked the sides around her to warm her. To his amazement, she fell into his arms and nuzzled her face beneath the fold of his coat. Her wild curls tickled his chin. Her flowery scent drifted up to him, wrapping him in feelings of warm spring and new things and he couldn't resist. He dipped his head and buried his face in the soft caress of those wild curls.

Was that a kiss? Austin's breath warmed the top of Dulcie's head and she felt certain that his lips were buried in her hair. Wild pleasure surged through her and she sighed with relief as his warmth enveloped her. She wanted nothing more than to snuggle deeper into his arms. She'd cooled off too quickly and now she couldn't stop her body's natural reaction. She trembled and shook for a long while before she could finally take a deep breath. Austin smelled crisp and clean, like leather and soap. Burying her nose deeper beneath his jacket she held on tighter. His arms held her close. Secure.

She felt safer in Austin's arms than she'd ever felt in her life and it had nothing to do with the body heat they were sharing. It was all about his kindness, the way his jaw set in a determined line when he thought of the missing women. How he constantly underestimated his abilities. The clear blue honesty in his gaze when he told Bea Yazzie he'd do his best to find her granddaughter.

Austin was authentic. Real. Not full of boastful pride or overbearing assurance. He might not believe it, but he could right wrongs and make the world safe for women who never felt that way. She rested her cheek against his chest and listened to the steady, strong beat of his heart.

"I'm sorry." His words rumbled deep in his chest and startled her. "I should never have brought you here. I wish I'd put two and two together and taken you back to Durango after McGuire's call. Whitehorse has a finger in every crime in the area. If I was thinking right, I would have realized he'd send men right away."

She did not want to rise from the comfort of his arms so she didn't. It felt too good. "It would have been a waste of time to take me back to Durango. Time we don't have. Now we know Whitehorse is involved."

"We know more than that. I'm pretty sure those two who followed us are Walter Benally and Bob Carson."

This time she raised slightly to look at him. "Are you sure?"

He nodded. "I recognized Benally's voice. It's distinctive. He's Whitehorse's muscle and does all the man's dirty work. I just tried to serve a search warrant on Bob Carson. His mother claimed he's running with Benally so I suspected he was Benally's partner. I was right."

She eased back down onto his chest and into the comfort of his arms. "Does that mean you can identify them and arrest them for shooting at you?"

"I'll try...if we get out of here in one piece. They're waiting for us up in the parking lot. I've been going over the trail in my mind, trying to think of a way I might climb up the rocks and get to my Jeep without a fight."

"Maybe they'll give up and go home."

He made a humorous sound that rumbled deep in his chest. Dulcie liked it.

"They will be sitting in their warm car all night. I think we'll give up before they do."

She shook her head. "You'll figure out something."

He stilled. "You sound complacent for someone about to spend a freezing fall night at the bottom of a canyon."

Complacent. No, not complacent. Content. She was content in the arms of a man who made her feel safe, who instilled confidence in her, who made her feel like all the world could sometimes be good. A man whose heart belonged to someone else and maybe always would. That thought should have frightened her and sent her scurrying away to the security of her own corner. But it didn't. She had never felt like this before, never even thought she could feel this way about a man. For a little while…or maybe even just for as long as it lasted, she would enjoy this moment.

"Not complacent," she murmured, trying to express herself without giving away too much. "Confident. I'm confident you'll find a way."

His chest rose with a deep breath. "You shouldn't have confidence in me, Dulcie, especially not after what just happened. I slipped up, made…mistakes."

Something in his tone struck a nerve with her. It sounded like pain—a deep, ongoing pain. "*We* took a risk today, yes. But it wasn't a mistake and it was worth it."

He gave a sharp shake of his head. "Risks are never worth it."

This time, Dulcie rose to meet his gaze. His Stetson shadowed his face and she couldn't see his blue eyes, the ones that said so much more than his words expressed. She wished she could see them, see how deep the pain went. But she didn't need to. She knew exactly what troubled him.

"This isn't about me, is it? It's about Abey."

He didn't answer. Instead, he shifted and moved so he could climb to his feet. Dulcie scooted back, gave him room. She felt the cold emptiness the minute he stood. It wasn't fair. She'd told him her life story, confided things she'd told no one, not even her counselors. But he wouldn't talk to her about his wife. Her disappointment went bone deep. But this wasn't about her, about the attraction she felt for him and he obviously sensed. This was about something more.

"I'm not the only one who trusts you. You inspire

confidence in other women. Susan's grandmother is certain you will find her granddaughter."

Refusing to look her way, he shook his head. "Determination doesn't always lead to success. I'm determined to find these men. Doesn't mean I'll succeed."

"But it makes it more likely. You won't give up easily, Austin, and people sense that in you. No matter how many times I had setbacks in my counseling, I pulled myself together and went back. I never let it stop me and look where I am now."

Spinning quickly, he fixed her with a hard look. "Yeah, look at you now. Frozen every time a man gets close."

She caught her breath. His words pierced again. Hurt washed over her so deep, she couldn't even speak. The ache must have shown on her face because Austin shook his head again, spun and walked away to stand at the edge of the passage. Once there, he shoved his hands in his pockets and his back was stiff and straight.

Dulcie felt the misery go through her like a wave of heat. She let it sweep through because she'd learned one thing in all her years of counseling... Once the pain washed away all the false hopes and crushed dreams, the truth would stand bright and brilliant. So she let the waves of pain clear away her ragged emotions until one thing rang true.

She shied away from men. She had trouble trusting them... All except for one.

"Not you," she whispered to his rigid back. "I trust you."

With that admission came another. Just because she

trusted him, was willing to share her life stories with him, didn't mean he felt the same way. Just because he was special to her didn't mean she was to him. She wished she could be special to him, wished he felt he could trust her the way she trusted him. She wanted to be the one to crack the impenetrable wall around his heart. But it was a foolish wish. He'd just proven that. She could never be the kind of woman his wife was, a strong person, a leader among her people…and now a martyr to lost hope. Dulcie wasn't sure any woman could live up to Austin's memories of his dead wife. And that made her even sadder.

The cold bit into her body. She needed to get moving, get her blood circulating. Austin was right. Tonight would be miserable…especially now that she wouldn't be in his warm arms. She paced back and forth, stretching her stiff legs and swinging her arms. It didn't help much. The cold was piercing. It wasn't long before she was shivering again.

Austin came back. She barely glanced his way. She kept up her brisk pacing.

He slid his fingertips back in his pockets. "Dulcie, I didn't mean…"

"Yes, you did." She glanced up. Her words caught him off guard because he froze in surprise, fingertips still linked in his front pockets.

She shook her head. "You don't have to apologize for speaking the truth. Besides, I shouldn't have pushed you for info you don't want to share."

He released a heavy breath. "It's not that I don't want to share. After she died, I talked to counselors until I couldn't talk anymore. I know how to do that. That's not the problem. Being here on the reservation has been hard. I've tried to block the memories from my mind, to concentrate on our investigation, but I can't. Meeting Bea Yazzie was especially hard." He looked down and around. Any place but at her. "Abey's grandmother was a weaver too, but when Abey was a teenager, she wanted nothing to do with it. After she found out she was pregnant, she decided that she'd stop all her volunteer work, slow down and make the time to learn the craft. She was spending long hours at her grandmother's hogan. That night she stayed until after dark and that road…" He shook his head. "I should have made her stay at the hogan and not let her drive home on that lonely stretch."

This time Dulcie didn't stifle her thoughts. He'd been unkind twice, so this time she thought it only fair if she spoke the truth back to him. "From what little you've told me," she said in a low voice, "I don't know if you could tell Abey what to do. It sounds like she had a mind of her own."

She caught him off guard again. His jerked his fingers free from his pockets and his blue eyes flashed in the shadows. He obviously didn't like her pointing out the truth. His sharp reaction told her that. She was glad. She might not be the one to break down the barriers around his heart, but he didn't need to live with a guilty conscience. That's one gift she might be able to give him.

"I should have said more, done more."

She shook her head. "We have that in common too. I thought if I could just reach that mother in California, I could save those little girls. It didn't work."

"Why not? Why didn't God honor your commitment and your struggles? For that matter, why did He let a woman and an innocent babe die like that, in the middle of a dark road alone and afraid?"

She shook her head slowly. "I've asked myself a similar question over and over again. Why couldn't God make my dad love me? Why couldn't Daddy just let go of the anger and love us?"

He pinned that piercing blue gaze on her. "I hope you got answers because I didn't."

"Oh, I got an answer and I'm sure you did too. You probably just didn't like it."

He glared at her. She could barely see his features in the dark but the pale moon, partially covered by clouds, still reflected off the hard set of his jaw.

"Sin is here, Austin. From the moment the angels turned away from God, sin entered the world. Bad things happen to good and innocent people. God weeps but He allows it to happen so we'll understand that His mercy is our only hope. He's the source of all good and our best reason to go on. *Romans* 9:23 says it perfectly. 'And that he might make known the riches of his glory on the vessels of mercy, which he had afore prepared unto glory.'"

She met his doubting gaze. "We were prepared for glory, Austin. That means we're unique. Special and loved. I cling to that every time I feel defeated. It's hard to hear His still, quiet voice in the world we live in. But He's there, listening, whispering in our hearts." She paused and looked up at the sky, at the brilliant bright stars. "Maybe the Navajo have it right living way out here. It strips away all our mechanical tools and illusions of power. His glory surrounds us in the skies and stars, so close we can almost touch them. I think it's easier to hear His quiet voice here because there's nothing to block out the sound and nowhere to hide."

The moon finally came from behind the cloud. She glanced back at Austin. His jaw was set and his blue eyes were hard and angry beneath the brim of his hat. The smooth line of his jaw tightened even more and the cleft in his chin twitched. He turned and stalked to the front of the passage.

With a heavy heart, Dulcie began pacing again. She was so cold, her teeth chattered.

Austin ran back to her, his voice pitched low. "Someone is coming down the path with a light." He grabbed her arms and pushed her toward one of the T-shaped openings into another room. "With that light, they'll be able to see right down this passage. Go deeper. But be careful. One wrong move and the wall could come tumbling down on you."

Dulcie gingerly stepped over the lip of the doorway and crouched down in the corner. Austin followed. They turned back to look through the doorway just as light flashed down the passageway they'd just vacated. The light beam swayed from corner to corner.

"Hey, you two, come out of there before you freeze. Let's go get warm."

The light flicked away. Dulcie and Austin stared at each other as Bea Yazzie's low voice echoed through the ruins.

SEVEN

Austin motioned Dulcie to wait while he checked outside. Sure enough, the old woman stood on the other side of the fence, her dog seated beside her.

"Come on. It's safe."

Dulcie scrambled out of the cramped space and they moved down the passage into the opening. Austin had to help Dulcie over the fence, a sure sign of her cold, numb state. When they reached the older woman, she shook her head. "You should not go to the ancient ones' houses where you will freeze. Why did you not come back to me when those two left?"

"How did you know they were following us?" Dulcie's teeth chattered when she spoke.

Bea clicked her tongue. "Those two…they sounded like a team of horses galloping down the trail, arguing and carrying on. I waited a long time after they left to come find you."

"We didn't want them to bother you, ma'am. They may be noisy but they're dangerous."

"Yes, I heard the gunshot. Fools." The vigorous shaking of her head showed even in the shadowy light of the moon. "Come on. I made you some Navajo tea. It will help."

They climbed the trail, the older woman moving ahead of both them. Their bodies and limbs were sluggish from the cold. When they entered the hogan, a battery-operated lamp sat on the table, casting a white glow over the single room. The cast-iron stove in the middle of the hogan radiated heat. Austin's face and fingers immediately tingled. He couldn't imagine how Dulcie was feeling. Bea handed her a heavy Navajo blanket and pushed a chair from the table closer to the stove.

"Sit. Both of you, sit."

Austin helped Dulcie tug the blanket around her as Bea poured a mug of tea. Dulcie wrapped cold fingers around the steaming cup and sniffed the liquid.

"What is it?"

Austin pulled another chair close to her and sat down. "An herbal tea made from a local plant. It's called greenthread. Go ahead and drink. It's full of antioxidants and good for you."

"I don't care how good it is for me. It's warm." She flashed him a little smile. Her dark eyebrows rose in an expressive gesture and her long curls bounced against her cheeks. Although she'd just spent four hours in the freezing winter temperatures, she looked wonderful. He couldn't turn away from her brown-eyed gaze or her peach-colored lips as she sipped the tea. Thankfully, Bea handed him a blanket and a mug.

He drank his tea and let the heat from the fire sink in.

His harsh words echoed through his mind. He felt bad about what he'd said to Dulcie, almost accused her of being weak and useless. She'd probed a painful wound and he'd lashed out…unthinking. It was cruel and he regretted it. But she seemed to handle it better than he did. She was over it by the time he'd returned and even spun it back on him with truths he couldn't deny.

Was she right? Did they have many things in common, like a need to save the world? It was why he joined the sheriff's department in the first place, to help make a difference. But when he'd lost Abey, he'd felt useless and thought he'd given up the notion of making a difference. But here he was again, trapped in a hogan at the bottom of a canyon with men waiting for him above… all because he thought he could help a frightened waif-like woman with the same need to help. He believed that need was dead…along with his faith in God. But he was wrong. Obviously, he hadn't given up all hope. He still had a sliver of faith that the Lord meant him to do some good and Dulcie had sensed it, had dragged it out of him. Otherwise they wouldn't be here now.

If she was right about that, maybe the rest of what she said was true too. Maybe they were prepared for glory. Maybe the Lord had plans for them…for him. He certainly hoped so. Or else all his efforts to help Dulcie would end tomorrow morning.

The old woman pulled more blankets off a shelf, and Dulcie helped her arrange them into pallets near the stove. When they finished, Dulcie grasped her hand. "Thank you. I don't think I could have lasted out there through the night."

The old woman nodded her head. "Tonight, you sleep. Tomorrow will take care of itself."

Yes, tomorrow will take care of itself. As he settled in his pallet near the warm stove, one last thought drifted through his mind. *Please, Lord, don't let me fail her.*

Austin opened his eyes slowly. With his senses tuned to any sounds outside the hogan, he hadn't slept well, and he had a crick in his neck.

Bea was already up. Water boiled in the kettle on the stove for more Navajo tea as she mixed bread in a wooden bowl. She pulled large pieces of the dough loose and dropped them into a cast-iron skillet next to the kettle. The bread sizzled and the smell of pork stew drifted over the air. His stomach grumbled without warning.

"You need to eat," Susan's grandmother said with a chuckle. "When you see people on the trail, then you can go. Those fools won't touch you when others are around. They are cowards who don't want to get caught."

Austin smiled, amazed at the older lady's wisdom. She might have led a secluded life but she was one smart woman. Dulcie stirred and rose from her pallet. She asked how she could help. Bea told her to set the table and she found bowls and spoons on a shelf. When the fry bread was done, the elder lady spooned the stew into bowls and they ate on their pallets, close to the fire.

All the while, Dulcie's gaze wandered back to the loom. It wasn't long before Bea explained how it worked. She talked about her craft, how so much of a Navajo woman's heart and soul went into the making of a Navajo blanket. Austin listened and remembered

Abey's grandmother saying the same things. But this time the words didn't hurt.

Maybe Dulcie was right. Talking about the good things eased the pain of the bad.

About nine o'clock, he heard voices and looked out to see two couples making their way down the trail to the ruins.

"It's time." He stood and Dulcie helped him fold and stack all the blankets.

Dulcie turned and grasped Bea's hands. "Thank you. We wouldn't have made it through the night. You saved our lives."

The old woman nodded. "Yes, it is because he is the one who will find my granddaughter and bring her home." She turned to Austin. "Do not forget. I am waiting."

Two days ago, her words would have filled Austin with guilt and trepidation. But today, thanks to Dulcie, he half believed the old woman.

And that he might make known the riches of his glory on the vessels of mercy, which he had afore prepared unto glory.

We're unique. Special and loved. Dulcie's favorite scripture and words echoed in his ears. Austin wanted to believe. He needed to. People were counting on him.

He nodded toward the old woman. "Thank you."

She nodded back at him with a half smile that made Austin think she understood everything he was thinking. He gave her another quick dip of his head and moved toward the door .

Dulcie gripped the older woman's hands and said, "May I come and visit you again?"

"Yes. Come. I'll teach you more about the weaving."

Dulcie's responding smile was beautiful. Austin could have stood by the door forever, watching her dote on the older woman. But they had a long trek ahead of them. He forced himself to turn and walk away.

Austin stepped outside to check the trail and the lookout above them before he allowed Dulcie outside. Bea stood in the door of her hogan and waved as they headed up the trail. Dulcie seemed particularly subdued. Just before they moved out of sight, Dulcie turned back and waved. When she saw Austin watching her, she gave him a shrug. "I never had a grandmother."

That thought occupied his mind for a long while during the trek up the trail. He couldn't imagine not having a grandmother. Even though his lived far away, he knew Abey's grandmother well. She used to laugh at his jokes so he saved all the corny ones to tell her. The memory pleased him.

Now that they were rested and fed, the trek up wasn't as difficult as he expected. No one met them coming down. He wished someone had. He would have liked to ask about the parking lot, how many cars and who was there. But they met no one descending, and sooner than he expected they drew near the top. As they reached a corner, he told Dulcie to pause.

"Wait here for me. I'm going to leave the trail and climb over those rocks so I can see the parking lot. If it's clear, I'll call you."

Dulcie's warm, soft hand grabbed his, made him want to linger, but she gave it a squeeze and let go. "Be careful."

He climbed the steep hillside and crept over the large boulders marking the parking lot. He lay flat and peeked over the edge. The lights of a tribal police car flashed. The vehicle was pulled up behind his Jeep and a tall, slender, familiar figure walked around it. Austin sighed with relief. Rising to his feet, he waved Dulcie up and climbed the rest of the way.

"*Ya ta he*, brother."

Cade Hatalhe paused and turned, "*Ya ta he*. It's good to see you walking around in one piece."

"You don't know how glad I am to see you too."

Cade shook his head. "We got a report of a gunshot. When I saw your Jeep, I was sure I was going to climb down there and find you with a hole in your head."

"You almost did."

"Your lieutenant has been burning up the airwaves looking for you. What kind of trouble are you in now, brother?"

Dulcie came running up. Both men turned. She'd spent the night on the dirt floor of a hogan and hid in dusty ruins and still, she looked amazing. Her russet curls shone in the early-morning sun, and her eyes were expressive and sincere as she examined Cade. Austin felt a sense of pride…that was quickly squelched when he caught Cade's speculative glance.

"Who is this?"

"Dulcie Parker, this is Deputy Cade Hatalhe from the tribal police. He's my…" Austin hesitated.

"Clan brother," Cade finished for him. "Even though my clan sister is gone, I still claim this one." He nudged his head in Austin's direction. A thankful flush of warmth washed through Austin. He didn't deserve Cade's faithfulness or affection. He'd walked away, turned his back on the people here, people who loved him, who were hurting too. He shouldn't have left. They could have shared the pain, walked the path of grief together. He felt humbled that they still wanted him back. And he owed that realization to the slim red-headed waif beside him.

"Our office got a report of two men on the trail and a gunshot early this morning. I was headed out here to talk to Bea Yazzie so I got the order to look around."

"Are you working the Yazzie girl's case?"

"Yeah, not that I'm getting very far, very fast. I've hit another dead end. Any idea who fired at you?"

"Walter Benally and Bob Carson."

Cade shook his head. "Benally. That one is trouble. I heard he was running with a man from Durango but I didn't know who. So why are they after you, brother?"

Austin trusted Cade implicitly, so he related the events that had led them to the canyon. Cade listened with an occasional shake of his head and a muted sound of frustration.

"You know if Benally is involved, Whitehorse is the one giving him direction."

Austin nodded. "I suspect Whitehorse's bar is one place the victims all have in common. They snatch the girls from different locations but I'm sure they spend time at The Round Up bar. The girls would probably recognize Carson and Benally from the bar and not be on their guard. It would make their kidnapping easier. I'm going to pay it a visit."

"So, you think Susan Yazzie didn't just run off. You think she's one of the ring's victims?"

"I think so, yes."

Cade looked away, frustration in his taut movement. "I thought she might have gotten tied up in that situation with Judy Begay and her stepfather, but once he was arrested, I believed it was over. I had no information about this ring."

"And I had no clue about Susan. The ring has been suppressing info. We've discovered that much for sure."

Cade shook his head. "This is bigger than all our departments. You need to report this to the FBI office in Farmington. We can use their resources."

"As soon as I get Dulcie someplace safe, I'm going to The Round Up."

"It's my case too. Let me help. I'll go to Whitehorse's place while you take care of Dulcie and go to the FBI. I'll put out an APB for Carson and Benally. Any idea what those men are driving?"

"No, we were already in the canyon when they arrived. But Carson's mother said he owned a white panel van. As soon as I have cell reception, I'll contact my lieutenant. See if he can't get Carson's registration. We'll get the ball rolling on our end too."

"Interdepartmental cooperation." The tall man grinned. "May be a first."

"Let's hope it's not the last. Be careful at The Round Up. You could be walking into trouble. Whitehorse and his cronies know they're suspects. There's no telling what they might do."

"I'll tread carefully." Cade patted Austin's shoulder. "In the meantime, get to Farmington. This case is crossing too many jurisdictions and we need help. Ask for Agent Bostwick. He's our contact."

"Will do."

"I'll follow you until the turnoff to Whitehorse's place. I want to make sure those two aren't waiting to ambush you on the road."

"Good idea."

Cade waved. "It was nice meeting you, Ms. Parker." He headed to his vehicle. Austin took his keys from his pocket and they loaded into his Jeep.

They pulled out of the parking lot onto the main road. When they drew closer to the highway and phone reception, Austin's phone buzzed with consistent messages. "I suspect my lieutenant has been trying to reach me." His wry tone made Dulcie smile.

He punched the connect button on his steering wheel and called McGuire. When his supervisor answered, his voice was taut. "You'd better have a good excuse for not checking in for the last twenty-four hours."

Austin shook his head. "How about getting shot at and trapped at the bottom of a canyon? Is that a good excuse?"

McGuire made a frustrated sound. "I knew something was wrong. This shouldn't have happened. I need to know where you and Ms. Parker are at all times."

"Agreed. I won't make that mistake again."

"So what did you discover in the canyon?"

Austin filled him in on all that happened, right up to the meeting with Cade.

"Carson's mother was right. He's neck-deep in serious trouble. Listen, she also said he owned a panel van. Can you check his vehicle registration and get me a license plate ASAP? I want to get the info to Cade before he heads to Whitehorse's place."

"I'm on it now. I'll also contact the tribal police chief, and both the New Mexico and Colorado state police with the info. Your friend Cade is right. It's time to bring this case out into the open."

He clicked off and silence hung over the Jeep's cab. Austin glanced Dulcie's way and saw a small frown creasing the space between her expressive brows.

"What's wrong?"

"There are still so many unanswered questions. We don't know the leader of this group. Or where they take the girls. So many pieces of the operation are unsolved. I'd feel better if we could provide the FBI with answers... at least with the evidence I've already accumulated."

Austin shook his head. "Haven't you had enough? You've been threatened, almost kidnapped and now shot at. How much more do you want to experience before you say stop?"

"I keep thinking about those girls, about Susan Yazzie."

"It's been two months since they murdered Judy Begay. If they have Susan, she's probably been transported out of the area already."

"Maybe, but you said yourself there haven't been any more disappearances since Judy's death. Isn't it possible they stopped everything, waiting to see if Matt Kutchner would talk?"

"He hasn't. Never said a word about the ring. We

didn't have a clue that there was a bigger operation going on."

"Exactly. They promised him something. I don't know what they could offer him. He'll spend the rest of his life in jail."

"That's exactly what they offered him. His life. A gang this powerful could easily arrange to have him killed in prison."

Dulcie released a heavy breath. "You're right…and they've frightened Doris Begay into silence too. We have to find the leader, Austin, and make sure we stop this gang."

"We will. Once the FBI gets involved, more resources will be at our fingertips. We'll find them."

"That's why we need to retrieve my information."

She studied him, a hopeful expression in her gaze.

"You want me to take you back to my house."

"Do you think we can?"

Austin shook his head. "Aren't you afraid? We just spent the night in hiding."

A sweet smile floated over her lips, a tender, soft look that went straight to his heart. "I told you, you make everyone feel safe. You make *me* feel stronger."

He didn't like acknowledging that her words made him kind of happy, a little warm inside so he didn't answer. It wasn't long before his phone rang again. McGuire had Carson's license plate number.

"Everyone's on high alert. I made sure Deputy Hatahle's department was informed. He has the plate number too. We've got every law enforcement department in the Four Corners area looking for those two."

"Good. Since we're covered, we'd like to go back to my place and fetch all of Dulcie's info for the FBI."

"Probably not a bad idea. But with all of this gang's resources, they might have your address. I'll send Bolton up ahead of you to make sure the area is clear."

"Thanks. That makes me feel better."

"Just remember to stay in touch. The gang's game is out in the open and that will make them desperate. They'll want to escape and they won't care who they take down in the process. If I don't have constant contact from you, I'll be sending my men to find you." He clicked off.

Not long after Austin called his lieutenant, Cade flashed his lights.

"Cade is giving me the all-clear signal before he turns."

Dulcie watched as the deputy's cruiser pulled off the main highway. "Do you think Benally and Carson were waiting for us somewhere on the road and Cade scared them away?"

"I don't know. I think it's more likely the tourists did a good job of that. Benally and Carson couldn't afford to have witnesses to our murders. Cade's backup made sure they left us alone."

Dulcie's heart hammered. "Do you really think that's what they're trying to do, murder us?"

"It might have been their intention just to frighten us away, much like Delacroix tried to do to you, but once Carson fired that shot, they had to find us. They knew if I escaped there'd be an APB on them. Firing on an officer of the law is a criminal offense I can testify about."

She eased back around in her seat. The road twisted and they left the vast plains and began to climb the hills. "I'm relieved it's out in the open now. We can go forward with the investigation. No more skulking around and hiding."

Austin lifted a one-shouldered shrug. "We still need to stay in the shadows. You heard McGuire. They're desperate now. Carson and Benally will be on the run. There's no telling what risks they might take and the rest of the gang will cover their tracks, making sure none of the evidence leads to them."

"Surely they can't expect to keep their activities a secret. We know what they're doing."

"Yes, but we only have suspicions. We don't have one shred of evidence that will stand up in court. We'll be able to identify Carson and Benally, but neither of us can say for sure who fired the shot or what connection they have to the missing girls. All we did was drive Carson and Benally to desperate measures."

Everything Austin said was true. Dulcie wanted to argue, but she couldn't. His words only confirmed her deep-seated need to get back to her research. "Maybe we pushed them out into the open, but we also have more pieces of the puzzle. I suspect that Vonetta uses her position to identify the at-risk girls. Joey Delacroix proved himself a good soldier by keeping an eye on me. He probably also used his position with the city to suppress information about the crimes. Deputy Shaw loses reports and convolutes the already difficult communication between law enforcement agencies. Whitehorse's men do all the dirty work and kidnap the victims. But once they've been taken, Whitehorse wouldn't be foolish enough to hold them at his place of business, would he?"

Austin shook his head. "He's a snake, but he's not stupid."

"Do you think they transport them to their destination immediately?"

Austin was silent as he considered. "They take them from all over the Four Corners area, but the kidnappings happened at relatively frequent times. They wouldn't have time to transport them individually between snatches. I think there has to be a holding place of some sort."

"Or places. They'd have to move them around. That's the connection I have to find. I'm sure that will take us straight to their leader."

He gave her a quick sideways glance...then another.

She studied him. "What?"

"We're hours away from pulling in all the FBI's resources, but you still feel like you're the one who has to do something."

She didn't know what to say to that.

A soft smile slipped over his lips.

"Never leave a woman or child behind, even when your own life is threatened, right?"

"Unless I get frightened and can't move...like you said."

"Dulcie, I'm sorry. I was angry. I don't handle talking about Abey very well. Honestly, I admire your devotion."

"But..."

"But nothing. Just believe what I say."

Despite his words, she knew there was an add-on to

that statement. She felt the need to help, to do something, to take action. But every time the chips were down she became a prisoner of her own body. She didn't understand it. The Lord had led her out of her horrible situation, had helped her grow and find some peace. So why did He let this start again? Why did He allow the fear to control her? Was He trying to teach her something more? Was there something else she needed to understand?

Please, Lord, make me understand. Let me know what You want of me.

No answers came to her and so they drove silently into the mountains, straight into the dark clouds ahead of them. They climbed the foothills beside Mesa Verde and snowflakes started to fall. The streets of Durango were wet and slushy, piled high with the fallen snow from the day before. The drastic climate change between the desert floor and the mountain community surprised Dulcie. Once again, she marveled at this unique corner of God's creation. By the time they reached Austin's home, the snowfall was steadily increasing. She was glad when they finally pulled to a stop at the cabin. Officer Bolton was waiting for them. He came to Austin's window. "Everything's clear. No sign of anyone. Not even tracks in the snow when I first arrived."

"Thanks, Bolton."

The man waved and headed back to his car. Austin parked his Jeep near the walkway and they hurried inside. Austin rubbed his hands together and gave her that soft, rueful smile. "I still only have frozen pizza.

I can microwave that and some coffee while you gather your files. We need to get back on the road as soon as possible."

That smile wrapped itself around her heart and tugged. She couldn't stop from responding to it. How could she? He was apologizing for his home and his lack of hospitality when all she wanted was to curl up on the couch and stay forever. His home made her comfortable…he made her comfortable.

How had she come to this place? She'd found a man who gave her hope, made her want to walk beside him, to sit with him in front of his fire and fight the bad guys. He made her feel like they could do anything, be partners for life, fight the good fight. They could be the dynamic duo crime fighters. The thought made her smile too. But this wonderful, handsome lawman deserved a true warrior, a strong woman like his wife, not the weak, frightened shell she turned into when faced with her fears. He wanted…was holding out for that kind of woman.

That thought made her turn away from his kind features and his soft smile. "Sure. That sounds good."

"Move as quickly as you can. We need to get back on the road."

She hurried up the stairs, not daring to look back, or to dwell on the image of the two of them on the couch in front of the fire eating pizza. It was too good of an image to hold on to. She couldn't afford to keep those kinds of images. They would make letting go of him even more difficult.

She slid her computer and her notes in her case and

pulled the bag's strap over her shoulder. The smell of pizza drifted up to her. A glance in the mirror showed her that her night in the damp air had turned her hair into a frizzy, wild mane. But she didn't have time to mess with it. Pulling the strap higher, she headed downstairs.

Austin walked toward her, travel mugs in one hand and a foil-wrapped paper plate with pizzas in the other.

His thoughtfulness…everything he did pleased her, made her smile. "Pizza and hot coffee? Perfect."

He gestured to the door. "If you take this plate, I'll carry your satchel."

He stepped in closer to hand over the food. Reaching up, she tried to gather her untamed hair into a knot.

"Don't do that."

She halted. His blue-eyed gaze covered her hair with a look so possessive…so loving, her breath caught. She felt beautiful and worthy in all the right ways. He was close, so close his lips were inches away. He leaned closer. This…this was what it was like to be wanted by this man…to be treasured by him. She needed more of that feeling, craved his kiss, his lips on hers. Then the look faded. That was the moment he remembered the woman between them, the woman she could never match.

He stepped back, looked away and cleared his throat. "It doesn't suit you. You don't need some kind of 'uniform' to hide the real you."

Handing her the plate, he then spun and stalked to the door. Dulcie's knees gave out and she almost slumped to the couch.

His words still echoed inside her. He didn't really see her now, frizzy hair and all. He saw the woman she could be.

That thought pleased her. She could be that person. She might never have this man or be worthy of him, but she would become the woman he thought she could be. She would make it her goal. With new resolve, she followed him to the door.

Austin's cell phone rang. He punched the speaker button with his thumb as he opened the door. "I've got my hands full so you are on speaker but we're on our way."

McGuire's deep voice echoed across the room. "Sit down, Austin, I have more bad news."

He froze and turned to face her.

McGuire's loud voice pierced the air between them. "Cade's been shot. He was attacked shortly after he arrived at The Round Up. There was a gunfight and he was hit. He's being air vacced to the hospital as we speak."

Dulcie cried out. Austin closed his eyes in frustration. "I knew I shouldn't have let him go alone."

"Apparently he saw Carson's white van as soon as he arrived and called for backup. He didn't go in alone. But they attacked him before reinforcements arrived."

"How bad is it?"

"Pretty bad. I'm heading to the hospital now."

Emotions washed across Austin's face, fear, anger and then frustration. She knew exactly what he was feeling. He was stuck here with her when he wanted to be at Cade's side. "We can go. I'll go with you."

He gave his head an abrupt shake. "We can't risk exposing you to the gang."

McGuire heard their conversation because he said, "Actually, that's the only good news I have for you. Cade's backup arrived shortly after he was shot. They took three men into custody. Benally, Carson and Whitehorse are in handcuffs. Their rampage is over."

Relief washed through Dulcie. "You have to go, Austin. You need to be by Cade's side."

McGuire spoke again. "I've contacted the FBI. Their men are on the way from Farmington. But I'll send Bolton back up there to watch over Dulcie until they arrive."

Emotions battled on Austin's face, so Dulcie took the decision out of his hands. She gently pulled the phone from his hand. "Thank you, Lieutenant McGuire. I would appreciate Officer Bolton's presence."

"I'll send him back. He just arrived. He'll be there in thirty minutes. But Austin needs to get going."

The lieutenant clicked off. Austin stood there motionless, his body frozen stiff with indecision.

Dulcie gestured to the door. "Go. Your clan brother needs you. I'll stay here and find the link I've been looking for. I want to have all my information ready when the FBI men arrive. We'll get them, Austin. I promise."

He nodded. Maybe he saw conviction in her features because he believed her, the woman he secretly thought was soft and weak. He seemed to understand that she would give every breath in her body to find the link... and she would...for the sake of the captive women and for this man. His unspoken confidence in her made her feel special, strong…wonderful. For one breathless moment, he leaned toward her. Again, she thought he would kiss her. She wanted him to kiss her. But he straightened and walked to the door, leaving her feeling cold and alone.

"Don't open this for anyone except Bolton. He'll be here soon."

EIGHT

Snow was falling hard and wind whipped his vehicle sideways. Visibility was difficult on the icy roads. In all honesty, he should call McGuire and tell him to send Bolton home. This storm was getting too nasty to drive in. But the truth was he didn't want to stop. He wanted to get as far from Dulcie as possible because he was feeling things he didn't want to feel...like admiration and tenderness. He didn't want to remember how her dark eyes and sweet lips softened when he looked at her, how each time she opened up like a soft rose unfurling. A copper rose.

He shook his head. Those kinds of thoughts should be reserved for his wife. So, he ran from Dulcie and the things she made him feel. Yes, he wanted to be by Cade's side, but truthfully, he was running from his emotions.

He never thought he'd want another woman...a woman who was as different as night and day from Abey.

How could this have happened? How could he have *let* it happen? He stared at the white sheet of snow in front of him. The storm was slowing him down, making his trip worse. The vehicles he encountered crawled along the road. Bolton would surely be delayed and Dulcie would be alone. That thought chased away all others.

He wouldn't…couldn't leave Dulcie abandoned no matter how he felt. He had to stop running.

Punching the phone connection on his console, he called McGuire. "Tell Bolton to stay put. This storm is getting worse. It's too dangerous to travel up the mountain, and I can't leave Dulcie stranded. Keep me informed about Cade."

"I was just about to call you. Those two men we arrested who identified themselves as Benally and Carson lied. They had no ID on them, so it took a while to confirm. They're not the two we're looking for. They're Whitehorse's flunkies who gave the deputies those names to fool them and give Carson and Benally time to get away. They escaped in one of Whitehorse's vehicles…a white single-cab truck. We got the call out to search and it was spotted almost immediately. They were passing through Durango but they lost the cruiser following them."

An icy certainty settled over Austin. "They're headed up here. I'm going back to Dulcie."

"Be careful." McGuire's voice was taut with concern. "We just got notification to shut down the roads. We've had hourly bulletins and the storm has turned from bad to worse. Hopefully, we'll stop Carson and Benally at the roadblock."

"Unless they got through already."

McGuire was silent for a long while. "I'll repeat myself. Be careful. They know we're onto them. They'll do whatever it takes to keep the evidence out of our hands."

"I'll stay in touch."

Austin waited for a truck to pass then turned around slowly. The road was slushy but starting to get slick. He'd made the right decision returning to Dulcie. It wouldn't be long before this road would be impassable.

He slowed as he hit a curve. Lights far behind him flashed as he turned the corner. He was a bit surprised someone was on the road. He would have thought the roadblocks McGuire and the deputies implemented would have stopped all traffic coming out of Durango. The vehicle made him nervous, but the snow increased and he needed to concentrate on the curves. Next time he looked up, the lights were closer. The vehicle was definitely white. He couldn't tell the make. The snow was blinding and it was still too far away. He took the next curve faster than he wanted but he needed distance between him and the white car.

Despite his best efforts, the car gained on him… which told him the driver was moving faster than he should on this slick road. Moments later, it caught up. It was a white single-cab truck. Because of his angle of view, he couldn't see the face of the driver but he didn't need to. Only desperate men would drive the way they were in this storm.

He hit a straightaway on the road and the truck sped up so fast, it pulled up beside him in the lane of the on-coming traffic. Now he could clearly see two figures inside. Benally and Carson. He jammed on the gas and his Jeep shot forward. But the bigger engine of the vehicle easily caught up to him.

If they kept this up, he'd never be able to get far enough ahead to secure the house. Maybe he should go past his home, try to draw them away.

No, they could double back and find the house on their own. His best option was to slow them down, somehow disable their vehicle.

It wouldn't be difficult. The snow was coming down so hard, visibility was almost zero. Whatever he was going to do had to happen soon. They were coming up on a stretch of road with twists and turns and a nonexistent shoulder between the road and the guardrail. But what could he do? How could he slow them without risking his own safety? Maybe he could block the road and hold them off until help could arrive. It was the only way to keep Dulcie safe.

He lifted his foot off the accelerator and slowed to a crawl. He just needed an open space to turn his Jeep around without spinning on the slick road.

The truck zoomed up so fast, Austin didn't have time to turn around. He pressed the accelerator again, determined to get out of the path of the oncoming vehicle. But the white truck kept coming, close enough to see Benally in the driver's seat and Carson on the passenger side. Benally crossed into the path of oncoming traffic and pulled up beside Austin's vehicle. Then the man jerked his wheel and bumped the side of Austin's Jeep, pushing him toward the edge. He was trying to shove him off the road just like Delacroix!

Austin manhandled the swerving vehicle back onto

the road and jammed on the accelerator. He sped forward through another curve, barely keeping his Jeep on the icy road. Another bump like that and he might spin out.

He had to keep his distance. He sped down the road but the truck followed. Only a few feet of space separated the two cars running down the slick road at fifty miles an hour. If either of them lost control, they'd crash. With his eyes on his rearview mirror, Austin watched the white vehicle gain on him once again. He pressed the accelerator all the way to the floor. The Jeep barreled ahead putting a few more feet between them but not much.

"Idiots! We're going to crash." He mumbled the words out loud and realized that's exactly what Benally intended. He and Carson had nothing to lose. This was their last gambit. Their operation was broken. Whitehorse was arrested. Cade might not survive to testify against them. Austin and Dulcie were their only other witnesses. The criminals were going to make sure the two of them didn't live. They intended to kill him first, right here on the road.

Any hope of escape or slowing them down flew out the window. Gripping the wheel, he focused on the black strip of highway rapidly disappearing beneath the onslaught of the snowstorm. Surviving the next few miles would take all his concentration. His cell phone rang. He couldn't answer it and didn't even have time to wonder about who was calling. The ringing cut off, as if he'd lost reception. Probably because of the storm. The icy road was ahead of him. A curve was coming.

Please, Lord.

He barely had time to send up the words before he was leaning into the turn and slipping...sliding to the edge of the drop-off. At the last minute, his wheels caught and pulled him up the hill. Straight into the next curve.

He took a quick breath and looked in his mirror. The truck made the turn too, sliding into the other lane of traffic. Veering into that lane again helped Benally close the distance Austin had gained. Benally's vehicle took the curve better than Austin's lighter Jeep and closed on him. Austin pulled into the other lane, praying officers had stopped the oncoming traffic. He sent up another prayer as he hit the next curve and slid once again. This time the side of his car skimmed the guardrail. Sparks flashed in the dark air as metal ground against metal.

He glanced back. The heavier white vehicle took the corner better again, not even coming close to the rail. It gained more mileage, driving up so quickly, Austin was sure it would hit his bumper. He took his eyes off the mirror. The next curve came upon him fast. He barely had time to turn into it. He released the gas pedal, hoping to slow. He felt his vehicle sliding and suddenly... the truck bumped him from the back.

It was all the impetus his slipping Jeep needed. He slid across the road, broke through the guardrail, flew off and hurtled down a short, flat incline to the side of the mountain and a hundred foot drop-off.

Long after Austin left, Dulcie's mind kept wandering back, remembering the look in his eyes, the one that made her feel beautiful. She could see the shape of his lips, still feel the yearning to touch them with her own. The way he leaned in…and then the shuttering of his feelings. The cold remembrance of a woman Dulcie could never match.

That's what had stopped him from kissing her. He remembered Abey, her strength, her compassion. Dulcie could never match that, could never be that woman. She didn't even want to try anymore. But it felt good to know his feelings for her were strong. That she almost made him forget. That gave her hope for another man and a future. It wouldn't be Austin. She knew that. She also knew she would always compare any man to Austin. But at least now she had the knowledge that she was capable of love, that a man could ignite those feelings and she could respond. There was a time when she thought that wasn't possible. She would always be grateful to Austin for protecting her and awakening her womanly emotions, for making it feel safe to love and be loved.

But there were other women who were not safe, who needed protection. That's what Dulcie should concentrate on now, finding the location of Susan and the other missing women. The gang had to have a holding place. But where?

Rocky Mountain Dreams… Pierce's real estate company. Austin told her that Carson's mother said Pierce had handled the sale of her home. She said he was representing property all over the mountain. Could that be the answer? Was Pierce finding different locations all over the mountain, multiple places to move the girls from one to another? It made sense.

She pulled up the real estate sales and searched through the listings. Rocky Mountain Dreams had facilitated ten sales in the last month. There were six residential homes, two retail businesses in town and two pieces of property without buildings. She looked up the first one and clicked on the satellite app to get a visual. It was hard to see through the pine trees, but there were no buildings on that property or the other.

Next she looked up the retail buildings. They were smack-dab in the middle of downtown Silverton. Even though they were large vacant buildings, neither place was a good location for holding women as prisoners. They were far too visible.

Frustrated, she made herself a mug of hot chocolate. The wind kicked up and howled. It sounded like the storm had turned into a blizzard. She thought of Austin traveling down the mountain and wanted to call but first, she wanted to have good information, something positive for him to hang on to as he watched Cade fight for his life.

Settling down on the sofa again, she pulled up the satellite photos of the remaining six homes Pierce's company had sold. Each of them had buildings, cabins or larger houses...making them viable locations to hide victims. But how could they know which one? Would they just walk up, knock on the door and start asking questions?

She dug deeper, looking for the buyers of each property. A company called Equine Properties purchased two of them. Satellite images showed that both locations had smaller cabins with no outlying buildings, something like what Austin found on the Carson property. More suitable to hunting or weekend places rather than homes. Interesting.

Equine Properties' website listed itself as a small renovation company, ready to buy fixer-uppers. There was another blurb about turning renovations into dream vacation homes. But when she went to look up the owners, she found nothing.

"Who are you, Equine Properties?" Saying the name out loud made something click.

Wait...equine meant horses. Could Whitehorse be Equine Properties? She opened files in the county clerk's office and found nothing. She dug deeper and finally found the registration DBA for Equine Properties. Owner and sole proprietor...John Whitehorse.

Dulcie leaped to her feet and whooped. "I got you, you snake! I got you!"

This was the evidence they were searching for, enough proof to fill out a search warrant for the cabins. She wrote the addresses of the two locations on a sheet of notepaper. Snatching up her phone, she dialed Austin's number.

It rang and rang until his voice mail clicked on. "Austin, I have the link. Whitehorse has a shell company buying property around Silverton from Pierce. They're working together! Two of the places look like the Carson cabin you described to me, and I've written down their addresses. I'm sure they're using those places to hide their victims. I hope that's enough probable cause for a search warrant… Okay. Call me when you get this."

She hung up. In the sudden silence, the storm howled. It was terrible and Austin was driving in it. For the first time a tingle of fear climbed up her spine. She hurried up the stairs to the loft to look out. All she could see through the window was a sheet of snow, falling so fast she could barely make out the trees around the property. Austin was outside…in this? Had he made it down the mountain?

Her heart stopped. *Will he make it back up to me? Am I stranded?*

The blood pounded in her temples as she ran downstairs to check the weather on the internet, but she couldn't connect. The storm had knocked out the internet. She tried her cell phone reception. Nothing. She was all alone in a blizzard. Panic started to sweep through her. Suddenly, the sound of a car engine made her pause. Had Deputy Bolton arrived?

She ran upstairs again to look down on the yard. A white truck she didn't recognize pulled to a stop in front of the house. Definitely not the deputy. Two men in dark clothing stepped out. She couldn't see their faces, but she saw enough to know they were strangers.

Panic surged through her and she ran back downstairs. There was no knock on the door or calling out. Instead, gunfire exploded and hit the door. The solid wood splintered, sending pieces across the room. Dulcie screamed and dove for the couch.

They had to be members of the gang and they were here to get her. They concentrated their shots around the dead bolt. They were shooting out the lock! Any minute they'd be inside. She looked around desperately searching for somewhere to hide. There was no place. No nook or cranny. Just Austin's wide-open home, the place she'd loved from the minute she saw it. Now it would be her trap.

Her notes! She needed to hide her notes. Most likely they'd take her to one of the locations she'd just discovered. Austin needed to know where to find her. Her mind stumbled at the thought. But what if they had no intention of kidnapping her? What if they meant to kill her? Her heart banged in her chest for one long moment before clarity came to her.

If they killed her, then Austin needed the evidence to stop them. She ripped the note off the pad and stuffed it under the sofa cushion just as the metal dead bolt flew out of the door and across the room.

A large hand reached in through the hole and turned the lock on the handle. The door slammed open. Two men stepped inside and marched toward her. Numbness crept over her. Everything slipped into slow motion. She wanted to scream. Wanted to turn and run…somewhere…anywhere. But she couldn't move. Couldn't make a sound as one of them grabbed her arm and shook her.

"Good thing you're making it easy for us," one of them ground out. "After all the trouble you've caused, I wasn't of a mind to be nice." He had sandy hair and light-colored eyes.

The other man had darker coloring. "You just gonna stand there and let us take you?"

Dulcie didn't answer, couldn't. She was paralyzed but her mind still raced. She recognized the raspy voice they heard echoing in the ruins at Canyon de Chelly. This man was Benally.

He spun her around. Something tight and sharp pulled her hands together. She heard the distinctive zip of a plastic tie. "Maybe you don't fight 'cause you think Deputy Turner is coming to your rescue."

The sandy-haired man laughed. "Yeah, Benally. That's what she thinks. Why she's not even moving."

How did Carson and Benally escape the Navajo police custody? She wanted to ask, thought the words, even tried to shape them with her lips, but still, she was paralyzed.

Benally shoved her bound arms, turned her around to face him and pulled her close. His dark eyes glinted with something cold and cruel. "Let me take care of that right now. Turner isn't coming. Not now. Not ever. We pushed his car off a cliff into a canyon where if they ever find him, he'll be crammed so tight in that tin-can Jeep of his, they won't know where he ends and the metal begins."

For the first time since they'd entered, Dulcie was able to make a sound. She whimpered a mournful cry. Then her knees gave out. Benally caught her and threw her over his shoulder. Carson laughed all the way out the door.

NINE

Austin's Jeep landed with a bone-jarring thud. His airbag exploded in his face, momentarily stunning him. But the vehicle didn't stop. It was still rolling down the flat incline toward the drop-off. He couldn't see what was ahead, but he knew there was a hundred-foot cliff at the end of his slide. If he didn't get out, he'd be hurtling over it too. He gripped the steering wheel. Through the side window, snow flew by as his Jeep continued to plow through the deep drifts. They slowed his momentum but still, he needed to stop or get out before his Jeep reached the cliff.

Struggling against the airbag, he tried to touch his seat belt. Suddenly, the vehicle dipped into a ditch and lurched to a stop. Austin jerked forward but stayed cushioned by the seat belt and the airbag.

He sat motionless for a moment or two. His chest hurt from his slam into the seat belt. A corner of his neck burned where the belt had sliced him. But he had stopped and he was alive.

The nose of his Jeep was pointing downward. He

could hear the hissing of his hot engine melting the snow. At least he hoped that was the hissing sound.

Please God, don't let the engine be damaged. But the most important thing was that he was no longer headed toward the cliff. He leaned his head back against the seat and took a deep breath.

Thank You, Lord. Thank You.

Relief swept over him and a thousand unrelated thoughts jumbled his mind. He was glad to be alive. A few months ago, he didn't want to live. He'd wished for the numbness of death, but now...now he wanted to live. Dulcie's lovely, distinctive image with those dark eyes and wild hair flashed into his mind. How could he have ever thought she wasn't attractive?

She was unique. Tender but strong in her own way. She wasn't a warrior like Abey, but she was a capable fighter. She battled her way through her fears. Conquered her own desire to hide and pushed forward every time...even when *he* wanted to run away. She was special. He should have told her so and held her close when she trembled. He wished he'd kissed her when he left her at the cabin...and at the ruins. Instead, he'd criticized her. Said hurtful things and made her feel less than she was.

Please, Lord, give me the chance to tell her how I really feel. Let me show her how much she amazes me.

His thoughts came to a stuttering halt. Benally and Carson had just pushed him off the cliff. Now no one stood between Dulcie and those animals. He had to get on the road and back to her!

Galvanized into action, he released the seat belt. He

couldn't move with the airbag. He needed to cut it open, but he couldn't reach his pocket knife. The engine had stalled, but the key was still in the ignition. He shut it off and pulled out the key. Positioning it between his knuckles, he punched the key into the airbag holes at the bottom to enlarge them. It took three punches before the key finally pierced and deflated the bag. When he could move, he pushed on the door.

Cold, fresh air rushed in, but he couldn't open it more. The depth and weight of the snow he'd plowed through was piled against it and had it jammed. Finally, free of the airbag, he shoved the seat back. The extra room gave him the space to turn and push both feet against the door. It swung wide and he tumbled out, landing in the soft snow. He lay for a moment, letting the flakes fall on his face, once more thanking the Lord for his safety.

But he had to get going. He climbed to his feet and hurried to the front of his Jeep. The ditch he'd slid into wasn't deep. Apparently, the snow had slowed his descent enough so that the dip stopped his momentum. His bumper was crushed, but it looked as if his engine was intact.

Looking back up the slight incline, he could see that his Jeep had made a clear path for about twenty feet down. Snow was plowed away, down to black dirt in places, enough solid earth to give him traction. The guardrail where he came off the road lay broken and spread out over the boulders of the drop-off. It wasn't much of an incline, just about six feet, and a rough enough landing to trigger his airbag. But the four-wheel drive of his Jeep could make the climb up the incline to the road…if he could get it started and out of the ditch.

His legs wavered slightly as he realized how close he'd come to dropping to the bottom. But the Lord had been merciful. Now if he could just get his engine running again…

He ran to the back of the Jeep and pulled a hammer out of the toolbox. He pounded the plastic dash to break it open and release the airbag. After pulling it loose, he tossed the apparatus to the snow, climbed back in and put the key into the ignition.

Please, Lord.

The engine turned over. Laughing with relief, he shifted his four-wheel drive into Reverse and slowly gave it gas. The vehicle shifted but slid back into place. He sped up again. This time the car moved very little and mud flew back behind the Jeep.

The wheels were spinning, not catching in the slick mud and snow. The Jeep needed traction to pull out of the ditch. He looked around. About ten feet away, a snag, a dead tree trunk, stuck its ragged edges up to the sky. Maybe he could get enough wood or bark off the trunk to give his wheels the gripping power they needed.

Grabbing his shovel from the toolbox, he slogged his way through the snow and dug around the tree. The trunk was old and weathered enough that he could pull bark and strips of wood loose and carry them back to the Jeep. All the while, a ticking clock counted off the minutes in his head.

Fifteen minutes from this location to his house. Another ten to break in. Benally and Carson were already at his house. How long could Dulcie hold out against them?

He refused to let his mind answer the question. Instead, he stepped up his pace. At last he thought he had enough bark and wood beneath all four tires. He jumped behind the wheel and turned over the ignition. His Jeep lurched and climbed slowly out of the ditch. When its nose pulled out, he let out a shout of relief.

But he still had to climb back up the hillside and over the rocky embankment. It wasn't steep but the snow continued to fall as the temperature dropped. Even now the spots of solid ground he'd seen were covered with snow and probably icing over.

Slowly but surely, he drove over his path of descent. He was aware of every second passing and the knowledge that if his Jeep slipped again, the ditch might not stop him. He could still slide over the edge of the cliff. He refused to let that thought take hold. Reversing over his trajectory took all of his concentration.

He reached his last hurdle…the rocky edge of the road's embankment. Moving even slower, he inched up. His tires hit the rocks and spun and spun. He released the sway bar and tried again. Finally, one rear wheel caught and climbed. He gunned the engine and pushed the transmission.

"Come on, old girl. I know you can do it."

His murmured words seemed to work. One wheel climbed over the bottom rocks, giving him more traction. Slowly, rock by rock, he bumped upward. All four wheels eventually worked their way over the rugged incline until he struck gravel at the edge of the road.

His back wheels spun again, kicking up mud and gravel but this time, his front wheels were on hard rock and pushed him. He angled the Jeep, hoping one rear tire would catch the asphalt and pull him completely off the muddy gravel. Metal screeched as the edge of the broken guardrail scraped along the side of his Jeep, but he didn't change his angle. As the last wheel slid over the rocks and the vehicle banged downward, his back tire hit pavement.

This time Austin let out a whoop as he pulled onto the highway. He grabbed his Stetson from the backseat where the airbag had knocked it, settled it in place then slammed the shifter into Drive. "Hang on, Dulcie! I'm coming!"

The numbness paralyzing Dulcie left in one long shiver. Her senses returned with an awareness of cold. She lay on the floor of the truck. Her hands were bound behind her. She had no coat. Carson and Benally had not bothered to cover her after they dumped her on the floor. They had the heater turned up but very little reached her. It all seemed to be coming out of the upper air vents. Shock began to wear off and her whole body trembled and shook with cold and fear.

Closing her eyes, she took several deep breaths and silently prayed.

Help me, Lord. Strengthen me. I let these men take me without a word. I didn't even cry out. I have to do something. No one else will come. Austin is dead.

Pain washed through Dulcie. Kind, strong but sensitive Austin was gone. That thought made her want to cry out. Losing such a vital, wonderful man hurt her more than she could bear. She felt like screaming in protest. Maybe even yelling at God.

Why did You let this happen? Why didn't You take me instead? He is so worthy...so wonderful. The world needs men like him!

She stifled a sob and let the tears fall. After a long while, her favorite scripture came to her.

And that he might make known the riches of his glory on the vessels of mercy, which he had afore prepared unto glory.

She didn't feel prepared for glory. She felt lost. Forgotten.

Why did You bring this man into my life to open my heart and then allow him to be taken away? Austin was right. You don't care.

More tears streamed down her cheeks but her hands were tied. She couldn't wipe them away, so she buried her face in the corner of the floorboard and silently cried.

Drained and empty, she lay there, her face hidden, her hands tingling from the tight bonds and her heart broken. In the emptiness of her soul, Carson and Benally's conversation drifted toward her.

"We can't transport all of them in this truck. The cops are probably lookin' for it."

All of *them*? Did that mean they still had some of the kidnapped women under their control?

"As soon as we get to Silverton, I'll drop you off at the cabin and get us a new vehicle."

Were they taking her to one of the cabins belonging to Whitehorse? She'd left the locations of the cabins on that note hidden beneath the cushions of Austin's couch.

But Austin was dead. It would take days for anyone to find the note...if ever.

"That chick Susan... Her broken arm will slow us down."

Susan was alive!

Benally's gravelly voice rumbled across the cab. "She won't slow us down for long. We'll get rid of her first chance we get."

Dulcie's heart pounded. They were going to kill Susan.

"Pierce won't like it if we dump her here in his hometown. He likes the operation kept far away from him."

"He won't have a choice. The operation is blown. He'll have to find us a vehicle or he'll be just as exposed as we are. He won't want that, and I guarantee you, if I go down, he'll go down with me."

Dulcie's heart stopped. Pierce *was* the head of the organization. She'd just heard it with her own ears and it became the proof they needed. But what good was that? She was as dead as Austin. To be a witness, she had to live...had to escape. But how?

Despair swept over her again. She felt bereft, abandoned.

Lord, I could use some of the riches You speak of in Your words. I claim Your promise! Show me a way to save these women... Please... Austin gave his life for them. Let me do this for him.

Fresh tears spilled out as Austin's smiling image flashed in her mind.

At that moment, the truck slid sideways. Carson cursed as Benally struggled with the wheel and they continued to slide. At last, the vehicle stopped and jerked back onto the asphalt.

Carson cursed again. "The sooner we get off this road, the better."

"Relax. The cabin's just a few miles ahead."

Carson's grunt of disapproval was his only response, and Benally didn't sound as confident as his words indicated. The storm had shaken both men...and maybe that was the answer.

Maybe this storm was the hand of God disrupting these men's plans. Perhaps their fear and struggles would give her an opportunity.

Faith means believing when all else has failed.

Senses that had been dulled by fear and hopelessness woke and tingled with awareness. *Please, Lord. Help my faith. Give me courage.*

The vehicle slid again and both men jerked. Benally cursed as he struggled with the wheel once more and Carson grasped the handhold above him while the other pressed against the dash. They tried to hide it, but both of these cruel, dangerous men were frightened. They had done horrible things—beaten people, kidnapped women, murdered one young girl and Austin—and yet, here they were, terrified by this storm.

They were just as susceptible to the hand of God as

she was…maybe more so because they didn't know or have His promise to cling to. So why had she become paralyzed with fear when they walked in the door of Austin's home?

She didn't know. Couldn't remember. She only knew she believed the Lord's promise now and she would watch and wait. Her moment was coming.

Benally pulled off the highway onto a dirt road. Dulcie felt and heard the soft crunch of heavy snow as they drove over the thick snowdrifts on the side of the highway. They traveled into the depths of the silent white forest for what seemed like hours but was probably only minutes.

"At last," Carson murmured.

With her hands behind her back, Dulcie couldn't rise enough to look out the windshield at what lay ahead of them, but Benally pulled the truck to a stop. Both men opened their car doors and a blast of frigid air flew inside, causing Dulcie to shiver.

Benally disappeared. Carson opened the door, grabbed her feet and dragged her out. She stood on weak legs that wobbled and threatened to collapse. Carson didn't give her a moment to gain her balance before he pulled her around the door into the full force of the wind. Snow like sharp pellets hit her face and snatched her breath. She turned her head away. Carson shoved her toward the cabin's door. Light flared in the dark interior. She tripped on the porch steps. Carson caught her upright and pushed her forward. She stumbled into a cabin almost as cold as outside. Carson slammed the door behind him.

To her left, Benally shoved wood into a freestanding iron stove. In the opposite corner, five women huddled beneath a single blanket. Dulcie's breath caught. She couldn't see clearly in the shadows, but she was fairly certain the woman in the center, cradling her arm against her, was Susan Yazzie. She recognized her from the photos she'd seen.

Carson shoved her toward the women. A thin metal chain ran under the blanket and was attached to a hook in the wall. All the women skittered away as Carson came closer. Their blanket covering shifted. Dulcie realized that the chain ran through bands around each woman's ankle, looped back and through the hook on the wall. A lock secured the chain ends together.

Her captor shoved her toward the women. "Sit down."

The women made room for her, huddling closer together. All of them were thin, their hair matted with grease and dirt. A few had bruises on their faces. Susan's arm was bent at an awkward angle, definitely broken. A dirty white tank top braced the arm and was tied around her neck. She looked uncomfortable and her features seemed permanently settled into a frown of pain.

Susan had been missing for almost two months. Dulcie had no idea how long the other women had been captives. But they were all in bad shape. She started to speak but Susan shook her head in an almost imperceptible movement.

Benally slammed the iron door of the stove closed. Flames appeared through the cracks of the old-fashioned potbellied stove and soon, heat drifted toward them. One woman groaned with relief and leaned toward it.

She quickly squelched the sound and sent a sharp glance in the men's direction, but neither one reacted. They seemed preoccupied.

"I need to get on the road." Benally's damaged voice grated across the room. "Come with me to the truck and get their food. After I'm gone, you can let them loose and feed them."

Carson nodded and followed him out. As soon as the door closed behind them Susan whispered, "Is it really you, Ms. Parker? I wasn't sure with your hair down like that. You look so different."

The thought of Austin and his words brought the hurt flooding to the surface again. She pinched her lips against the pain, then said, "I've been told that. But how do you know me? We've never met."

The young woman looked down, her features gripped in pain. "Judy talked about you all the time. Sometimes I waited in the car outside the clinic for her to finish her appointments. You always walked her and her mother to the door and stood there and waved. Like you were their friend. I always thought that was really nice. Judy deserved someone nice."

Dulcie gripped Susan's free hand. "You were with her when she died, weren't you?"

Her features flicked to angry life. "She didn't die. They murdered her. Her stepfather led us right to them. We never suspected he was a part of them. They paid him money. Cash for his own stepdaughter. She was so angry when she saw him take the wad of money, she ran at him. He said horrible things to her, called her names. She clawed his face and he pushed her off the cliff. Just

pushed her off like she was a bag of trash or something.
Benally and Carson were furious when Kutchner did
that. Said he'd cost them money, so they wanted his pay-
ment back. Kutchner refused so they started fighting,
throwing punches. I got shoved to the side and landed
on a huge rock." She lifted her arm slightly. "That's how
I got this. They beat Kutchner up and left him there, on
the side of the mountain without a ride." She shook her
head. "They should have pushed him off too."

"He's in jail, Susan. My friend Deputy Turner arrested him. His trial starts soon."

Susan sighed. "At least he's off the streets. We knew
they were lying low and hiding." She nudged her chin to
the door where Carson and Benally had exited. "Someone was going to take us away from here days ago but
they refused to pick us up. They said it was too dangerous. After that, Benally and Carson moved us twice,
from one cabin to another and now back here. We figured someone was looking for us. We hoped they would
come…" Her words dropped off into empty silence.

Dulcie looked at the other women. She didn't recognize any of them. She would have thought at least
one or two would have shown up in the police reports.
Shaw had done a great job of keeping the reports stifled. Five women, from different places, with different looks: three brunettes, one blond and one redhead
like Dulcie. All of them with varying ages. One looked
as young as fifteen. Dulcie's rage increased. "They've
kept all of you like this for two months?"

The women nodded. Susan spoke again. She seemed
to be their spokeswoman. "We thought…hoped that all

the moving meant the police were close. But now…" She stared at Dulcie. "Now that they've snatched you right off the streets, what hope do we have?"

She shook her head. "I wasn't just snatched, Susan. I was investigating the disappearances and got too close. They came after to me to shut me up, but the sheriff's department knows all about this ring. They…"

The door opened. Benally walked in. All the girls stiffened. Frustrated, Dulcie stopped talking and turned to face the man. He carried a large case of water bottles with boxes stacked on top. He set them on the table then pulled a handgun out of his jacket.

Dulcie shouldn't have been surprised but she was. She knew they had a gun because they'd shot the lock out of Austin's door. But when they'd taken her, they had not used a weapon. They didn't need one. She'd just stood frozen while they bound her and dragged her away. She looked at the frightened, haggard girls sitting around her and promised herself that would not happen again.

"Move back, girls." Carson gestured them away from the ring on the wall. They scooted as far back as the chain would allow. He opened the lock and they slipped free of the chain. They moved apart and tried to stretch their limbs.

Carson palmed his gun in one hand and with the other, lifted Dulcie to her feet and dragged her to the table where he placed the gun. Dulcie stared at it as he spun her around and slid a pocketknife between her hands. The zip tie slipped free. Blood rushed to her fingertips and immediately burned. Sharp pains shot through her shoulders and she shrugged them, forcing cramped muscles to move.

All the while, she kept her gaze on the gun. But she needn't have bothered. With her hands and arms numb, she couldn't grasp it even if Carson gave her the chance. But her moment would come. One way or another, she would set these girls free.

Her captor punched a hole in the plastic wrapping around the water bottles and pulled the tops off the boxes of granola bars. He shoved them at Dulcie. "Hand these out."

She obeyed even though her hands could barely grasp the bottles and bars. When she finished, she sat down with her own bottle of water and a granola bar. She could hardly force the food down but she didn't know when she might eat again and she needed her strength.

When she finished, she massaged her wrists. Cuts from the ties hurt like crazy, but she continued to work her wrists, trying to restore all movement. She was the healthiest and probably the strongest of the captives. If they were going to make a move, it had to come from her and she promised herself she would be ready.

Carson crossed to the cabinets, pulled a large old-fashioned transistor radio off the counter and returned to the table, where he placed the gun beside him once again. Then he began to fiddle with the radio's dials. Static filled the air. It was just the sound Dulcie needed to cover her movement as she sidled closer to the table.

The roads were so slick, Austin slowed to a crawl. He'd lost track of time during his efforts to get back on the road and the storm had knocked out all cell reception. All he knew for sure was that Benally and Carson were ahead of him. He prayed his sturdy home, with its high windows and strong doors would keep them out, keep Dulcie safe until he could get there. He even prayed that the storm would get worse, prevent them from reaching her. But as he arrived at the turnoff to his drive, the tire tracks leading up the dirt road told him the two men had traveled over it. He pulled into his yard, stopping where their tracks ended, and stared at his wooden door as it swung back and forth in the wind. Snow was piled on the tile of his entryway.

Demoralized, he climbed out of his cab and stomped through the almost knee-high snow. All of his efforts were for nothing. They'd blown away the lock of the door like it was paper. The lights were still on. The fire had burned to embers and Dulcie was gone. Her computer and files were missing too.

All of his fears settled over him like a frigid blanket. He had no idea where to go…where to look. She would disappear into the network they had been operating right under his nose. He'd failed…again.

He slumped to the stone hearth and hung his head. He should have known he would fail. All he'd ever wanted was to help people, to make a difference. And yet, he could not even save the most important women in his life. He was no hero. Never had been. The hope that had sprung to life inside him, the wish that maybe this time, he could make a difference, sputtered out and died. All of Dulcie's words about God's grace and the riches waiting for them were just words. If God existed, He was the same uncaring, unresponsive Creator Austin had come to know. He gripped his head as tears filled his eyes.

Dulcie didn't deserve this. She shouldn't have put her trust in him. But she had.

The words spilled out of him before he could stop them. "Lord, if You're out there. Help me help her. Don't let her be another victim."

No answering words came to him. No voice in the wilderness gave him courage. Shaking his head in disgust, he jerked off his hat and tossed it onto the sofa where it landed with a whoosh.

The edge of the cushion where his hat rested was tilted up, caught on its neighbor. He bent lower. Tucked beneath was a piece of paper, which he jerked free. It was a page from Dulcie's notepad with the words *Pierce's properties* at the top and two addresses below. Was this the connection Dulcie had been searching for, the places where the ring hid the kidnapped women? Inspiration struck and he pulled out his phone. He still had no reception but that last call he'd received had been from Dulcie. He was certain she'd called to tell him of her discovery but she was cut off. Still…she'd had enough presence of mind to hide this note from her captors. Hope and pride surged to life inside Austin.

If Pierce was the leader of the gang, then Benally and Carson were most certainly headed his way for help. If they all wanted to escape, their only option was to go through Silverton where they could wait out the storm and then go over the pass to Ouray. That had to be the direction they had taken…the place where he'd find Dulcie!

Austin strode to his broken door. After dragging a kitchen chair behind him, he secured the portal against the wind. Then ran through the stinging snow to his Jeep. The engine turned over. Austin said another silent *Thank You*. He wasn't sure if he was praying or if God would even answer. He only knew he was thankful. He spun the vehicle around and headed for the road.

Travel was slow going. Every mile was a struggle and with each one he gave thanks for getting another step closer to Dulcie. After what seemed like an hour, he saw the flashing lights of the police department's blockade on the other side of the road. They were stopping anyone from traveling down the mountain. But there was no blockade on his side. He was free to move forward. He hesitated for one moment, wondering if he should alert them. But his uncle's words about Pierce's connection to the local police department floated through his mind. Pierce had a strong influence in this small community. Austin didn't know how strong or how deep that influence went with the police. He couldn't trust them. He drove on, determined to reach the location of the closest cabin. If he didn't find her there, he'd go to the next and search until he did.

He drove through the almost empty streets of Silverton. Only a few cars were out and about. Just beyond the outskirts of the small mining town turned tourist-and-artist haven, Austin slowed. The road to the first cabin was close but it was difficult to find it when it was covered with at least three feet of snow. He had no cell phone reception to check his GPS but he had a map in his glove compartment. He could find it on the map, backtrack and estimate his mileage if necessary. He traveled a few more miles down the road until finally, afraid he'd missed the turnoff, he pulled to the side.

The storm had created a whiteout. Few people were driving but if he stopped, he could not be seen and might be hit. He needed to pull far off the road to check his map. He eased close to a pine, its branches laden with snow, and reached for the map.

Deep in the forest in front of him, headlights flashed. He paused and squinted through the trees. A white truck twisted and turned down a side road right before his eyes. He punched the switch on his lights off and watched in amazement as the vehicle crossed in front of him. He leaned forward, squinting through the blinding snow. Sure enough, the front fender of the truck was crushed on the right side…the side that had been used to push him off the road. He couldn't see the face of the driver but there was only one man in the cab.

Stunned, Austin leaned against the seat as amazement filtered through him. His descent down the hill… halting abruptly in a ditch before he went over the cliff, his Jeep's engine starting again, backing out and climbing onto the road. The paper beneath the cushion and now…one of Dulcie's kidnappers showing him the road to her location. Too many accidents. Too many perfectly shaped events to be coincidences. Was it possible God's hand had been with him all along?

The vehicle's driver paused at the road and turned

onto the highway, driving right past Austin without even slowing. He never saw Austin parked to the side.

No way were these coincidences. God was guiding him…had been guiding him every step of the way. Emotions he couldn't describe swept through him. All he could do was raise his gaze to the heavens.

"I'm sorry. I was wrong. I don't deserve Your forgiving grace but thank You for leading me to her."

He jammed the gear into Reverse, backed out and turned down the road. Keeping to the tracks left by the SUV gave him traction on the winding path. Always conscious of the minutes ticking by, Austin leaned into the steering wheel as if he could push the vehicle to go faster.

At long last, he glimpsed light through the trees. Hopefully, the howling storm wind would mask the sound of his Jeep. Still, he stopped far away and killed the engine. He could barely make out the frame of a window in a decrepit old cabin. Smoke curled up from the chimney and swirled in the windy gusts. He popped the Jeep's door open and the smell of wood smoke drifted toward him. The wind caught the door and pulled it wide with such force, it slammed back against his shoulder. He turned away from the biting, icy pellets trying to shred his face. After easing the car door closed, he turned and trudged through the woods toward the cabin. He stopped behind a tree for a long moment, trying to decide what to do next.

The cabin appeared to have only one way in. He had no idea how many men might be inside. He prayed Carson and Benally hadn't been joined by others from

Pierce's group. Thankfully, one man had driven away in the truck. A thought struck him. The missing man might be his way to get in. He pulled out his gun, checked his ammunition and moved forward.

He skirted the clearing in front so he could cross to the side of the building. Once there, he ducked around the corner and leaned into the cover of the building to escape the stinging snow.

Hopefully, the wind would be his friend. He took a deep breath and shouted into the gusts. "I need help out here."

His ploy worked. The wind picked up the sound of his voice and muffled it until it was barely audible. He held his breath and waited. Had they heard his cry for help inside? Did he need to say it again?

Just as he took another breath to shout again, the door swung open. A square of golden light spilled out onto the snow but no shadow covered it. Whoever opened the door was being cautious and stood to the side. Austin groaned loud enough to carry over the wind and waited. After a long while, the shadow of a man edged out from behind the wall…a dark gun was in his hand, clearly etched in the snow.

What should I do? Rush him? Or wait for him to step out? Austin's whole body tensed and his pulse pounded in his temples. If he waited much longer, the man would grow suspicious and close the door again.

The shadow leaned farther out. Austin could tell by the movement of his dusky head that he was searching the line of trees in front of the cabin. Suddenly, a black object hit the man in the back of the head. He jerked and moaned then collapsed on the threshold. The object landed in the snow outside the door. It was an old-fashioned transistor radio.

Austin studied the lumpy shadow. No one ran to the man's aid so Austin cautiously stepped out from behind the corner of the building. Bob Carson lay unconscious on the ground, half in the door and half out. His gun had fallen free from his lifeless fingers. Austin ran to the door, kicked the small pistol into the snow behind him and lunged into the cabin, his revolver poised in front of him.

Five frightened women, clinging to each other, stared at him from across the room. Dulcie stood beside a table a few feet away from them, her face drained of color.

"Austin! You're alive!"

TEN

Austin stood before her. She couldn't move. Couldn't say another word. Then he shoved his gun back into his shoulder holster. In two steps he was in front of her, his arms around her, binding her close to him. He felt very much alive. She couldn't quite believe it.

Reaching up, she touched his cold cheeks. "They told me you were dead."

"Not yet. Thanks be to God." He pulled her head down and buried his face in her hair. "And thanks to you. I found your note under the cushion."

She smiled. "I should have known you were alive. God would not have given you to me only to snatch you away."

He stared at her. His blue eyes dragged over her features as if he were memorizing them. At long last his gaze met hers. "I don't understand the strength of your faith. But I want to. There's so much I want to understand, but there's no time. Benally could return any moment. We have to get these women..." He paused and studied the group still huddled on the floor. "All of these women into my Jeep and get out of here before he returns." He paused. "Is that Susan Yazzie?"

"Yes, they've been holding her since Judy was murdered, holding all of them, moving them between the cabins here in Silverton. They knew we were looking for them." She grasped his upper arms. "Pierce is their leader, Austin. I heard Benally and Carson talking. Benally is on his way to Pierce now to get a vehicle large enough to transport all of us once the storm clears. They know we exposed their operation and they're running!" She hugged him tight. "We did it, Austin! We broke the ring."

He didn't seem to share her enthusiasm. He gave a quick shake of his head. "All that means right now is that Pierce and his men are more desperate than ever. We have to get away from here…someplace where we will all be safe until McGuire can get up here with reinforcements."

"Can't we go to the local police?"

"Not yet. Not until I can get word to McGuire about Pierce's connection. I don't know who he might be controlling in the local force."

Fear that had spilled out of her at the sight of Austin crept back in. "Where can we hide until then? Susan is hurt and all of them are weak. They need food and water and most of all a warm place."

"I think I have an idea. We just have to reach my uncle's house. Come on. Help me move Carson inside."

They hurried to where the man lay and dragged him inside. "Let's lift him into the chair. I want to secure him so he can't interfere while we load into my Jeep."

Dulcie helped lift the man's dead weight into the

wobbly chair. For a moment Dulcie thought it would collapse beneath him. Austin had to reach out and prop him up. He looked around for some way to tie him up.

One woman stepped forward, holding the chain and the padlock. "Here, use these. Chain him to the wall like he did to us."

Austin studied the chain then looked up into the face of the young woman.

Dulcie said, "Her name is Katharine. She lives in Cortez and she was taken two weeks before Kutchner killed Judy."

With a grim expression and a nod, he took the chain from Katharine's hands. "It's good to meet you, Katharine."

"Trust me, I'm thrilled to meet you, Deputy Turner."

He turned back to his task and dragged Carson toward the hook in the wall. "It sounds like you all did a lot of talking before I got here." He wound the chain around Carson, looped it through the hook and locked it in place. "That's a good thing because there's no time now for talk." Finished, he looked around. "All of you wait here while I get my Jeep. None of you are dressed warm enough to walk down there."

He started for the door and trepidation filled Dulcie. She grasped his arm. "Don't leave us unprotected."

Austin shook his head. "I kicked his gun in the snow. I don't know where it is."

He covered her hand with his own. "I'll be back in moments. I promise, Dulcie. I'll be right back."

A slight smile wavered over her lips. "There you go again, instilling confidence, being the hero."

Shaking his head, he said, "We definitely have to have a talk. The only hero around here is you." Then he spun and hurried out the door. Dulcie pushed it closed against the wind but left it open a crack. She couldn't bear to let him out of her sight. She braved the icy cold and stood in the opening, watching as he disappeared into the woods. She thought she heard an engine start, but it was difficult to hear over the roaring wind. Then lights flashed in the trees. Her heart leaped and she turned to the women. "Come on. He'll be here soon. Bring the blanket."

They hurried to her side. One of them wrapped the thin blanket around Susan's shoulders. Another supported her good arm. Their kindness in the face of such misery and torture warmed Dulcie's heart. One way or another, they had to get these poor souls to safety.

Austin pulled his Jeep as close to the door as possible and jumped out. Dulcie pushed the portal wide and the women piled out. Austin held the Jeep's door open and pulled the chair forward. They climbed into the narrow backseat. Two of the smallest girls had to sit on the lap of the others. Once they were situated, he helped Susan into the front seat and slammed the door. As soon as Austin was situated, he turned up the heat. Warm air flowed into the vehicle. "Hold on. It's going to be a rough ride."

The first curve they took pushed Susan to her side. She banged her injured arm against the door and a small groan escaped her.

"Here, let me help." Katharine loosened the blanket, folded it into a pad and placed it between Susan's shoulder and the door. When they took the next curve, she grimaced but the pain did not seem as bad.

The road was barely visible through the sleeting snow. Several times the Jeep slid over patches of ice. Austin shook his head. "The pavement won't be much better. Maybe we can follow the tracks Benally made on his way down. Let's just hope we don't see him coming back up."

They made it into town, slipping and sliding all the way. The streets of Silverton were empty. All sensible people were safely ensconced in their homes. Austin eased to a halt at a cross-street stop sign, mainly to check the depth of the snow on the street ahead of them. No tracks crossed the path and the snow was deep. "I don't want to risk getting caught in that. I'm going to back out and try another street."

He'd just reversed the car and turned in his seat when down the road, a large black SUV passed where they had been moments ago. "Austin, look. Someone else is out driving and it's a black SUV. Do you think it's Benally returning with Pierce?"

Austin eased the vehicle back out of view. "There's one way to find out."

Leaving the vehicle running, he opened the door and hurried to the sidewalk and around the corner of the building where he peeked out. Soon he came running back. "I can't be sure, but I think Benally is driving. I don't know who the other man is and…the SUV is definitely headed to the road we just came down."

Dulcie was silent for one long minute. "Do you think they saw us?"

"No. If they saw us, Benally would have recognized my Jeep and headed our way."

"How long before they find Carson and come back down?"

"I'm not sure. I just know we have to hurry." He turned the car around and took another route to his uncle's house.

Austin's mind raced as he negotiated the dangerous Silverton roads. Black ice was everywhere, and keeping the heavily loaded Jeep clear of the drifts and patches took all of his concentration. He searched his memories, trying to remember the day Benally was arrested. Everyone at the station knew his uncle worked on the railroad. Austin frequently talked about his uncle's adventures as an engineer on the steam locomotive line. Built in the 1800s, the narrow-gauge line ran from Silverton to Durango and was one of the biggest tourist attractions of the area. Austin tried to remember his conversations from that day. Had Austin talked about his uncle and his work? Would the criminal remember and draw the connection between them?

He didn't recall his conversations for sure, but he knew he couldn't risk hiding at his uncle's home. They had to find another place, one that was warm and would shelter the women. He knew a place and hoped his uncle would agree.

At long last, he turned onto his uncle's street. The small house sat on a slight incline above the road. Austin pulled to a stop and left the engine and the heater running. Then he dashed up the hill, slipping and sliding all the way, to pound on the door. Fortunately, lights were still blazing inside. His uncle was awake and he opened it very quickly.

"Austin…what are you doing here?" Uncle Butch stood in the doorway, his gray hair mussed, his flannel shirt untucked and fuzzy wool socks poking out from beneath his jeans.

"I don't have time to explain. I have six women in my Jeep. They're all victims of a trafficking ring operating here in our area. I've just rescued them from a cabin and I need a place to hide them and my vehicle."

"Hide? Don't be crazy. Let's call the police."

"Kent Pierce is the leader of the ring, Uncle Butch. After what you said about Pierce's influence over the local police, I don't know if I can trust them. I need to hide these women until men from my station can get up here. I thought about the railroad's roundhouse."

His uncle hesitated for a moment before he nodded decisively. "It's big enough for your vehicle and it has a couple of floor heaters. We can get the women secured there."

"We'll need your truck, too. I've got the women crammed into my Jeep and one of them is injured."

His uncle turned and pulled a key ring off a rack near the door. "Get it started. It'll be cold. I need to get my shoes."

"We also need blankets and food," Austin called out as his uncle moved down the hall.

"Grab what you need out of the kitchen and load it in the truck. I'll get the blankets."

Austin hurried to the garage and started his uncle's

truck. Then he pulled microwave soup cups, boxes of cereal and packaged cookies into a bag he found near the door. He snatched a container of bottled water up with one hand and headed toward the garage.

His uncle met him in the hall, his arms full of blankets and heavy towels. Nodding toward the microwave cups peeking out of the top of the bag, he said, "It's a good thing I'm widowed and have tons of microwave food lying around."

Austin grunted. "It doesn't fill me with confidence to know this is how you eat all the time."

He pushed open the garage door and held it for his uncle, who paused. "You should talk. Frozen pizza is better?"

Shaking his head, Austin nudged his chin toward the car. "We don't have time for this discussion."

They'd had this talk many times, the one where his uncle told him it was time to stop mourning, to move on with life. Celebrate Abey and all she did by living life to the fullest. His uncle had said many times how disappointed she would be with the half life Austin had been living. Before, Austin had no purpose, no reason to change...until Dulcie. Now he had everything to look forward to...if they survived the night.

"We need to move someone into your truck so we can make Susan more comfortable."

His uncle nodded. "I'll see you down there." He punched a button. The garage door lifted. Austin ran down the incline to his Jeep and opened Susan's door. "Come on. Let's get you better situated."

The young woman was weak. She struggled to get

out. Finally, Austin slid one arm behind her and another beneath her legs and lifted her out. His uncle parked beside him with his truck engine running. Butch opened the door and Austin slid Susan onto the front seat. Two other girls piled into the backseat and in seconds, both vehicles were headed down the road to the railroad's roundhouse.

He told Dulcie where they were going. "Okay," she said. "But what is a roundhouse?"

"It's a huge building where they do repairs and store the engines during the winter. Back in the day, the buildings were round so they could drive the engine in and around a circle and out. That's how they got their name."

"I see…a round house with round tracks."

"Exactly. The company doesn't run excursions down the narrow-gauge rails during the winter. It's far too icy and dangerous, so they store the engines and the railcars in the roundhouse."

Dulcie nodded and leaned forward as the large building loomed ahead of them. His uncle's truck stopped. He exited his vehicle, ran in front of the headlights, unlocked the tall metal doors blackened from the smoke of the coal-driven steam engines and then hurried back to his truck. He pulled inside and Austin followed, parking on the opposite side of one massive train.

Austin jumped out to help his uncle close the sliding door. "Go get the heat going for the women. I'll lock this."

His uncle nodded, then went back to where Dulcie and the others were helping Susan out of the truck. Austin didn't like the young woman's pale features and trembling posture. He was afraid she was going into shock. Apparently, Dulcie feared the same thing. He heard her tell the other women to make a pallet for her so they could get her warm.

A small area at the back served as the break room, complete with a microwave. Uncle Butch plugged in two large floor heaters. They had things under control, so Austin went to check out the building.

Steam engines filled the tall, long and somewhat narrow roundhouse. They'd barely had room to park their vehicles on the sides of the two huge train engines. He moved past the small break area to examine the rest of the building. The old roundhouse burned down in the 1980s and had been rebuilt. Only one original brick wall remained…and it was full of four-foot-high windows. Austin stared at the wall in dismay. No way could he secure those. If Pierce and gang figured out where they were hiding, it would be easy to break through those windows. He wouldn't be able to protect the women. One man and one gun against three men, probably heavily armed. There would be bloodshed.

Austin took a deep breath. But where else could they go? All they could do was keep the lights low and stay hidden. Hopefully, Pierce and his gang would not guess their location.

He moved back to the break area. The women sat on the floor, huddled around the heaters with blankets around their shoulders. Susan lay on a pallet. Dulcie pulled a foam cup of soup out of the microwave, blew on it and began to spoon-feed the young woman. A faint smile filtered over her lips.

The sight of Dulcie doing what she did best warmed Austin's heart. An hour ago, he'd thought she was lost. But here she was ministering to other women. God was good.

She was the only one without a blanket but his uncle had found her a bright yellow workman's jacket, two sizes too big for her. It hung over her hands but she'd rolled the cuffs up, out of her way. He shook his head. She wouldn't let anything like a little freezing cold impede her efforts to help these women.

How had he been so blind? He did not recognize that she was a warrior…different from Abey, but still a fighter. A champion of everyone except herself.

Austin decided then and there that if they survived tonight, he would spend the rest of his life showing her how wonderful, strong and beautiful she was.

Please, Lord. You came to me in my hour of need. Made me see how You've held me up. Pointed the way for me. Give me one last blessing. Let me spend the rest of my life showing Dulcie how valuable she is.

She looked up and caught him watching her. A sweet, soft smile filtered over her beautiful, coral lips…lips that were so expressive. They could go thin with displeasure and harden with determination. They were lips he wanted to kiss.

And please, Lord, if it is not Your plan for us to be together, let me kiss her just once.

His uncle walked toward him. Austin dragged his gaze away from Dulcie and nudged his chin toward the back of the building. When they had stepped away, he shook his head and kept his voice low. "I forgot about that wall with windows. They make this place indefensible."

Butch nodded. "But it's warm and safe for now and they need to rest."

Austin agreed and looked up at the rafters. A giant mechanized lift that slid back and forth was attached to the roof. A ladder led up to the arm. It was the highest point and offered the best view out the high windows across the building. "I should be able to see pretty far out the windows from up there. Call me if you need me."

Butch nodded and moved back to the women. Austin climbed the ladder to the top. Wrapping his arm under the rung, he leaned back to look out the window. He could see for several blocks over the city. Snow covered the streets in a blanket of white. Two black strips of tire tracks marked their way to the roundhouse. An easy trail to follow if Pierce and his gang saw them. What would he do if they found them?

For the second time that night, Austin hit a blank wall. No ideas came to him. He didn't know what their next step would be.

He inhaled and clung to his rediscovered faith. The Lord had pointed the way once. He would do it again.

Time passed. Austin could hear the women quietly talking, his uncle's low voice and the soft laughter of the women. Leave it to his uncle to lighten their hearts. Uncle Butch told them how the road from Durango through Silverton to Ouray was called the Million Dollar Highway because it cost a million dollars to build at the turn of the century. Others said they called it that because of the million dollars' worth of discarded gold ore that went into the dirt used in the road's building. Butch told them how, at times, the highway paralleled the narrow-gauge tracks and in weather like this, the tracks were safer.

Austin smiled with the women. He'd never appreciated his uncle more than tonight, when he'd jumped into danger without a second thought and tried to make these desperate women comfortable.

Austin's arm, clinging to the rung, was getting tired. He needed to climb down and rest for a while. Conserve his strength. He was about to begin his descent when the flash of faraway headlights caught his gaze.

He froze and watched as the lights flashed again, pointing straight down the cross street of the roundhouse's location. Austin's pulse pounded in his temples. Adrenaline surged through him as a black SUV turned down their street.

Kicked into gear, he clamored down the ladder and ran to the women. His uncle and Dulcie looked up. The fear must have shown on his face because his uncle came to where he stood in the shadows outside the circle. Dulcie followed close behind him.

"They've found us." He couldn't keep the stress out of his tone. "Is there someplace in this building with no windows where we can secure the women?"

"I think I know a way to get us out." Uncle Butch gestured them to follow him to a small yellow engine about twelve feet long. "This is a speeder. They use it to get to the Tacoma power plant. It's in here for repair, but I got it running yesterday. It's in tip-top shape."

"How does that help us?" The speeder had sliding doors and a small enclosed area behind the driver's seat. Outside the speeder on the back was a wide bar with a narrow platform. A small basket-trailer for equipment was hitched behind it.

"I think we can get all the women inside and drive the speeder. There's no road to the plant. They can't get there by car. Just railway tracks over a bridge and five more miles up the snow-covered mountain. They'll never make it by foot in this wind and snow. The building is warm and secure so we can hold out there until the storm passes."

Austin eyed the speeder. "Do you really think we can get all the women inside?"

"It'll be a tight squeeze, but what other choice do we have?"

Austin didn't have an answer for that.

His uncle went on. "There's just two problems. There's a stretch of open, flat meadow before we hit the bridge that crosses the river. Those men could follow the road above and maybe catch us before we get there. The speeder doesn't travel very fast. But the second issue is the bigger problem." His uncle paused.

Austin eyed his silent relative. "What's that?"

"You've got to open the doors, let the speeder get through and hopefully jump on the back. I can build up steam and get us out the door quickly, but you might find it difficult to hop on…and someone else could get on with you."

Austin studied the giant doors of the building and the small bar at the back of the speeder. He wrapped his hand around it. The black metal was just the right size for his grip. The metal platform at the bottom wasn't even wide enough for his feet. But he could manage.

"Let's do it."

Dulcie gasped. "Austin, you can't! Even if you get on, you'll be an easy target for those men and their guns. They could shoot you!"

"I don't think they will risk a shot this close in town where citizens might hear. So far, they've tried to keep all of this under the radar."

"Then let's call the police. If they don't want their presence known, they must be trying to avoid the authorities. That means it's safe to call them."

Austin shook his head. "You saw how Deputy Shaw disrupted the proper order of operations. It only takes one bad egg to send files missing or to release prisoners. We can't risk something like that happening." She started to protest but he grasped her arms and said, "You are witnesses and our only real evidence. Do you want these men to go free to do this again?" He shook his head. "We've got to get you out of here now." He turned to Butch. "Let's get them loaded and take as much blankets and food as we can carry. We don't know how long this storm will last."

Dulcie stepped close and grabbed the lapels of his jacket. "Austin...please don't do this."

He gripped her hands. They were cold. Her eyes were wide and her amazing lips were so close...and they trembled. He wanted to bend down and kiss her.

A loud bang at the back of the building made them both jerk.

Austin pushed her toward the group of women. "They're trying the back doors. In minutes they'll find those windows. Get moving!"

The women were loaded into the speeder. Katharine held Susan's arm and led her while the others carried the bags of food, water and the blankets. Butch was right. It was a tight squeeze but they managed to fit everyone in with spots for Dulcie and Austin. But she waited outside for him.

Butch gathered enough steam and released the brake. The engine crawled along the tracks to the tall doors. Austin met Dulcie and they walked behind the slow-moving vehicle.

His uncle leaned out of the open window on the driver's side. "Give me a few minutes to build up speed. I'll punch it the minute the door is wide enough. You let go of that door and grab on. I don't plan to lose you, nephew. You hear me?"

Austin gave him the thumbs-up sign. Dulcie reached for him. He grasped her hand and pulled his gun out of his holster and placed it in her open palm. "I want you to take this."

She shook her head. "I can't. I don't know what to do with it."

He pointed to the lock. "Flip this open. It's the safety. Then point and pull the trigger. You probably won't hit anything, but you'll scare them."

"I can't, Austin. I'm afraid of guns. I'll freeze up again." She gave another shake of her head.

"Take it. If these men find a way to get to the power plant and I'm not there, Uncle Butch will need it."

Her lips parted. Now. Now was the time for the kiss he'd been wanting since that first night in her apartment when she walked in with her wild hair, distinctive brows and sensitive mouth. He ran his hand over her soft curls, gripped her head and pulled her close…

Glass shattered at the back of the building.

They were in!

He shoved Dulcie toward the speeder and ran past his uncle to the front of the building.

"They're here. Go!"

His uncle nodded. Austin reached the large metal sliding doors and looked back. Dulcie had climbed in. He unlocked the door and shoved it wide. His uncle nodded again and released the brake. The speeder shot forward. Austin stepped close as it moved past him. He grasped the black metal bar. It jerked him off his feet and dragged him as the speeder moved out of the building. It still slow enough he was able to gain his footing. He hopped, trying to jump on the narrow platform. Just as the speeder took off, he gained footing on the back and pulled himself up.

Then he heard a shout. Carson ran toward them from the back of the building. Obviously Pierce and Benally found him at the cabin and set him free. Austin kicked him away, but he grabbed the basket at the back and tumbled into it.

Dulcie caught her breath as Carson tumbled into the flat basket attached to the speeder. Carson recovered quickly from his side tumble into the carrier and struggled to come to his knees. The basket wouldn't support the weight of the man so it dipped and swayed. He lost his balance several times. That gave Austin time to react. He bent behind the back of the speeder, out of Dulcie's vision.

All the women were turned, looking out the window. "He's pulling pins from the bar attached to the trailer." Waves of relief swept through Dulcie at Katharine's announcement.

Carson reacted too. Balancing on one knee, he lunged forward and snatched at Austin as he leaned over. Carson's growled shout echoed over the noise of the speeder engine and the women screamed.

Austin jerked back, pin in hand. Carson cried out in surprise as the basket carrier fell away. The connecting bar hit the tracks and tipped the carrier end over end, sending the man flying. He bounced, landed flat and didn't move as the speeder rushed down the tracks.

A collective sigh of relief flowed through the small cabin. Austin gave them a thumbs-up through the back window. But Dulcie wasn't satisfied. The storm still raged. Sleet bit into Austin's face and hands. He had to be freezing. She wanted…needed him inside with the rest of them. She faced the front as the speeder pulled away from the rail yard. They were still too close to the road but there had to be a wide, safe spot to stop so Austin could climb inside.

They all watched the railroad yard fall farther and farther behind. Dulcie thought they might make a safe getaway. Then she saw men run from the building and the black SUV pull onto the street, headlights flashing along the empty road.

She leaned toward Butch. "They just got into their car and drove away. Can they follow us?"

He nodded. "The highway runs on that flat space above us."

Dulcie glanced up the rocky cliff. A wide swath was cut out of the rock, wide enough for a two-lane highway. "But you said they couldn't reach us at the power plant. Where do the tracks pull away from the highway?"

He nudged his chin ahead. "Look up there, where that rocky hill crosses the tracks."

The tracks ran right through the middle of an outcropping with large boulders piled high on each side. "Just beyond that, a bridge crosses the Animas River. From there we're safely on the other side of the river away from the road."

She glanced back. Austin still gripped the bar, his features set as he ducked his head away from the flurry of icy snow striking his face. "Can't you go any faster? He's freezing."

"This is as fast as this little engine can take us. Austin's strong. He can hang on a little longer."

Yes, but could she? She relied on Austin. Counted on him. Needed him to lift her spirits, to give her courage and hope. She even had thoughts of staying in his house and filling the walls with beautiful treasures. She'd dared to dream of making it a home.

She loved Austin. Not just counted on him. Loved him. She had feelings for him from the moment she'd met him. For the first time in her life, she'd eased back on the throttle of energy and devotion that drove her to protect, to keep everyone and everything within her reach safe. She thought of the future, of what life could be like without the constant threat of loss or danger and she wanted it. Riding in the speeder with death so close behind them, Austin needed her help, and once again, she could do nothing.

The gun felt heavy in her hands. Abey would have known how to use it, wouldn't have hesitated to step forward to protect Austin. But it sat cold, heavy and deadly in Dulcie's hands.

She shook her head in frustration and looked ahead. The outcropping of rocks was only a few feet ahead. Butch said once they were past it, they would be free.

Please, Lord. Push us beyond those rocks.

They entered the narrow gap between the rocky boulders and were almost through it when a dark figure leaped from the side of the outcropping and lunged across the space. The women screamed but Dulcie lost her breath. The familiar paralysis of fear crept over her. She stood transfixed as the figure missed his footing on the speeder but latched on to Austin. The two of them struggled for a few moments. Austin punched and pushed to free himself, but the man hung on. Finally, unable to sustain his grip with the man dragging him down, Austin lost his hold and they both tumbled away, rolling through the snow.

The man was the first to gain his footing and marched toward Austin's prone figure. Dulcie recognized the determined features of Walter Benally. He grasped Austin by the coat, jerked him up and swung. His meaty fist connected with Austin's jaw. His head spun. Even in the dark, Dulcie saw blood spatter across the pristine snow.

Benally had the advantage of surprise and weight

against Austin. Benally punched him again. Austin appeared almost senseless from the blows. Now he hung like a dead weight from Benally's grip on his coat. Austin needed help. But Dulcie stood in helpless, frozen fear, the gun in her hand.

The gun. She had the means to help Austin…if only she could move.

Benally struck another blow. Dulcie whimpered with pain. Austin needed her. She had to move…had to do something.

And that he might make known the riches of his glory on the vessels of mercy, which he had afore prepared unto glory.

Dulcie wanted the riches promised to her. She wanted the chance of a future with Austin. She wanted to claim the Lord's promise. A tingling started in her fingertips. Warmth built until a heated wave swept through her. Frozen lips parted and she screamed, "Stop!"

Her cry pierced the speeder. Butch jumped and turned to her.

"Stop and let me off."

He pulled the brake and the little speeder slammed to a halt. Dulcie pushed the sliding door open, hopped out into the knee-deep snow. "Get these women to safety!"

She slammed the door shut with a strength she didn't know she had. Slogging through the snow, she headed back to where Austin and Benally struggled.

Austin seemed to have regained his senses. Benally straddled over him but Austin swung his leg out with enough force to send Benally sprawling. Austin lay there for one long moment before climbing to his feet and striding toward Benally's prone figure. The older man fought his way out of a deep drift. Austin reached him and landed a punch to the man's exposed jaw. Benally fell facedown but lunged out of the drift and tackled Austin. Both men rolled across the tracks. Benally cried out as his shoulder caught one iron bar. But they continued to roll through the snow, close to the edge of the tracks and the narrow path they created along the mountain wall. For the first time, Dulcie heard the roar of rushing water and realized the icy Animas River was below the edge of the outcropping…the edge Austin and Benally were still rolling toward.

Austin finally broke free. Stumbling forward, he reached for Benally. The man, unsteady on his feet, took a wide swing. Austin blocked it with his arm and punched with his right hand. Benally stumbled backward toward the edge.

His arms swung wide as his foot hit empty air. Austin jumped and lunged, reaching, trying to capture Benally's arm. But he missed. Benally fell with a cry that echoed over the stormy wind.

Dulcie caught her breath and stopped. She stood on the tracks, stunned, still far away from Austin as he leaned precariously over the edge.

A shot rang out, piercing the snow in a puffy flurry not five feet away from Austin. Dulcie looked up. A man with a long dress coat flapping around his legs stood above on the rocky outcropping of the highway. From her angle, Dulcie could see the black SUV, parked close to the edge. Smoke billowed out behind it. The engine was still running but the lights were off. They had raced along the road with no headlights so they could reach the outcropping undetected. That's how they'd beaten them to this point and how Benally had climbed down and lain in wait for Austin.

The man standing above them had to be Pierce. Even now he looked like the consummate businessman, not an assailant, taking aim again.

Austin was close to the edge of the cliff. Too close… and defenseless. She held his gun in her hand.

Austin ran for the protection of the boulders but he would never make it across the open space. Pierce fired another shot. This one hit the snow a few feet in front of Austin. The next shot would be closer.

Dulcie lifted the gun. Austin's words rang in her head. *Flip this open. It's the safety. Then point and pull the trigger. You probably won't hit anything, but you'll scare them.*

She braced her wrist, pointed and pulled. The shot echoed above the whine of the wind. The bullet went wide and hit the rocks below Pierce. The man jerked in surprise. Apparently, he had not seen Dulcie until that moment. She aimed and fired once more. The bullet pinged against the rocks. She fired again. Another ringing ricochet echoed over the icy wind. She fired one more time.

How many bullets did this gun hold? If she kept firing, would Austin make it to the safety of the rocks? What if she ran out of bullets and Pierce turned his aim on her? She stood out in the open with no protection.

It didn't matter if she was shot. Austin would be safe.

She pulled the trigger again and again. This time

sparks flashed as the bullets hit the rocks closer and closer to Pierce, so close, the man dropped his gun, spun and ran for the car.

Now that Dulcie was firing, she couldn't stop. She pulled the trigger one more time. The bullet pinged on the rocks. The lights on the SUV switched on. Dulcie pulled the trigger and the gun clicked...out of bullets. The engine of the SUV revved and Pierce screeched away from the outcropping.

The man who had harmed and destroyed so many women couldn't face his own risks.

Dulcie continued to pull the trigger even though the gun was out of bullets, and the SUV's headlights flashed along the rocky cliff headed back to town.

At long last, her gut reaction to fight back eased. She took a deep breath, dropped the gun to the rocky dirt beside the tracks and wiped her hands on her pants.

Austin marched toward her, purpose and intent in every step. As he drew closer, she saw his chin and cheek were bright red, scraped and bleeding.

"Are you all..."

He grasped her head, wound his fingers through her hair and pulled her toward him. His cold lips covered hers. They were firm, demanding, needy. They took everything from her...even her breath. She felt light-headed, weak. When she thought she couldn't give anymore, he broke the kiss.

Dulcie gasped for air and inhaled his soap-and-leather scent, the familiar scent that always sparked thoughts of warmth and comfort. She'd barely caught her breath when he tilted her head the other way and kissed her again. This time, his lips were soft, gentle, full of wonder as they shaped to hers, feeling their contours and depth. It was a loving kiss, one full of beauty and possession…a kiss of love.

When he finally released her, she stared into a gaze so full of tenderness, it took her breath away again.

Could it be? Was that love she saw in his eyes? Was it possible?

He gave a small shake of his head and his voice was low. "I promised myself if we lived through this, that would be the first thing I did."

She stared at him, his words barely penetrating the surprise filtering through her. "You…you wanted to kiss me like that?"

He nodded. "From the first minute you walked into your front room with your hair down."

"But you never…"

"I know. I fought every thought, every one of my natural needs. I even fought when the Lord told me to move forward. I was an idiot."

He lifted her head with a finger. "Almost as foolish as you, standing out here in the wide open, taking potshots at Pierce. Don't you know he could have killed you?"

She shook her head. "It didn't matter. You needed help."

He stopped the shake of her head with a firm but tender grasp. "And that, my foolish, brave girl, is why I love you. That's the most courageous thing I've ever seen."

His words jumbled in her head. Foolish. Brave. Courageous. Only one word clicked and had true meaning.

"You…you love me?"

"With all my heart, Dulcie Parker. Can you forgive me for being so blind, for not listening, for being prideful and angry and determined not to see and hear the signs the Lord sent to me?"

Once again, his words jumbled in her mind. "Signs? What signs?"

"You and your fierce, stubborn protection of the defenseless. Your determination to fight all your fears. You're a warrior woman in your own way."

"No…no, don't call me that. I'm nothing like Abey. Nothing. She was amazing."

He smoothed a hand over her wild, snow-dampened curls and shook his head. "Even in that you are wonderful. All the things I shared about Abey, all the ways I made her a star in my own mind…any other woman would have been jealous."

"I was." She ducked her head. "I am."

Tucking his thumbs beneath her chin, he lifted till her gaze met his once more. "Even in this you are incredible. You fight those feelings of envy with admiration. You could be angry or resentful but instead, you praise her and care about her memory. You value her strengths without ever recognizing that you have them too. You need to admire those traits in yourself, my lovely warrior."

She shivered as the truth of his words swept through her. This time she grasped his face and pulled his lips down to hers. This kiss was tentative, explorative… as if she didn't have the right to do it. But she grew bolder and kissed him as if he was hers. At last they broke off again.

Dulcie leaned her forehead against his. "Truth be told, I've wanted to kiss you from the first moment I saw that dimple in your chin. That's the only truth I know and I'm so glad you awakened those feelings in me."

Her words ended in a cold shiver.

"Trust me—I can't wait to explore those feelings. But first, we have to survive. We're three miles from town in the middle of a raging storm without transportation."

Dulcie shivered again and looked around at the empty path of the tracks that disappeared around a bend.

"What about Benally's body?"

"He won't bother us anymore. Come on. Let's go find our friends."

ELEVEN

Dulcie huddled close to Austin. They leaned into the wind and walked down the tracks in the direction the speeder had gone. Now that the danger was over, Dulcie felt the cold more than ever. They reached the outcropping and looked ahead. A narrow bridge crossed the river. On the other side sat the bright yellow speeder. Dulcie had never been happier to see anything… Well, maybe only a living Austin as he stood in the cabin door when she believed he was dead.

Grasping her hand, Austin tugged her forward and they ran across the bridge.

Butch threw the sliding door open. "I knew she'd save you."

As Austin helped Dulcie inside, the look he gave her warmed her body all the way through. "She saved me all right…in more ways than one."

As soon as Austin slid the door shut, Butch gunned the speeder and the pointed metal front plowed through the snow-covered tracks. They traveled more miles before a large brick building appeared in the distance.

Butch pointed to it. "They built the Tacoma power plant in 1905. I go there pretty regularly. I'm in charge of their speeder so I have my own keys to the facility. The main room hasn't many amenities but there's a control room that's nice and warm and I know for a fact, it has a microwave." Butch winked and the women laughed. Dulcie didn't know him very well but she was already beginning to love Austin's uncle Butch. She was certain they would be good friends.

He drove the speeder into a covered garage-type shed and they trudged through the knee-deep snow to the main building. Butch unlocked the doors and led the way upstairs to a narrow control room with complicated dials and monitors along one wall. On the opposite wall was a long desk below windows that looked across the river for a good view of the empty road.

They found the microwave and heated cups of soup for the women. Then they all settled on the floor next to each other and appreciated the warm room.

Austin ran a check of the building one more time before easing down to the ground next to Dulcie and leaning his back against the wall.

"I thought you'd be asleep by the time I got back."

She smiled at him and dropped her head on his shoulder. "I can't. My mind is spinning."

"What are you thinking about? I'm sure we're safe for now. Pierce and whoever is left in his gang are probably scrambling to find a way out of Silverton."

"I wasn't thinking about them. I was thinking… well…where do we go from here? What's next?"

He linked his fingers through hers and studied their

clasped hands. "There'll be a trial. Your agency will lose your leader."

She smiled. "I know all that. I'm not worried about the shelter or my work."

He leaned out slightly and gave her a look. "What's this? You're not worrying about someone else for a change?"

She squeezed his fingers. "No, I'm not. My work will not change, but I will. I don't want my life to go back to the way it was."

Lifting their clinched hands, he kissed the back of hers. "I think we both feel the same way."

She nodded. "I hoped so, but how do we change, Austin? Where do we begin?"

He let his head fall back against the wall and heaved a sigh. "I have no idea."

"Well, I know exactly what I want. I'm going back to visit Bea Yazzie at her hogan. I want to learn all about Navajo weavers."

She could feel his gaze on her but he didn't speak and she didn't dare meet his gaze. Would he agree or turn away from the path she could see so clearly ahead of her? Would their relationship be over before it even began?

At last she gained the courage to face him. "Will you go with me to visit her, Austin?"

A slow, sweet smile eased over his lips. "I would be honored." He kissed their clasped hands again.

She took a gradual, deep breath. "Would you do one more thing for me?"

A frown creased his brow. "If I can."

"Would you dig out the Navajo rug Abey's grandmother made and hang it on the wall below your front room windows?"

His smile faded. He was silent for a long, heart-stopping moment. Finally, he dipped his head. When he spoke, his voice was low. "It's time. I'll do it. But only if you'll help me. I'm not very good at hanging things."

Joy filled Dulcie's heart. She leaned in, kissed him again, then nestled her head in the crook of his neck. Safe in the shelter of his arms, she fell asleep.

When she woke, bright sunlight was flowing through the control-room windows. The storm had passed and the women were stirring. Butch was already up and had warmed soup in the microwave and passed out packages of fruit-and-nut bars.

Suddenly, Katharine rose to her feet and pointed across the river. "Look!"

A caravan of county patrol cars, blue lights flashing, followed a snowplow down the road to Silverton. All the women except Susan stood and cheered. Within minutes they were packed and loaded back into the speeder. It took time for the speeder's engine to heat up, but soon they were on the tracks headed to the engine roundhouse. When they were on the outskirts of town, cell phone reception returned to Austin's phone and he dialed McGuire.

"Am I glad to hear your voice." His supervisor's gruff tone echoed over the phone and throughout the speeder. "Where are you?"

Austin explained their situation and Pierce's involvement.

"Don't worry about him. I'll send men to his place and will keep the roadblocks in place. We'll get him. You just get yourself safely to the roundhouse."

Dulcie looked around at the women. Relief filled their features and brought tears to their eyes.

When Butch pulled the speeder into the open area of the railyard, flashing blue-and-red lights were everywhere. Ambulances, fire vehicles and police cars were all waiting to greet them. Dulcie even thought she recognized FBI agents in dark coats. The place was swarming.

Austin was the first one out of the speeder. McGuire rushed across the space and pulled him into a pounding embrace. "It's good to see you."

"It's good to be here. We almost didn't make it."

McGuire nodded. "It was a close call all the way around…for Cade, as well. But I'm happy to report he came out of surgery and doctors expect a full recovery. In addition, my men found Carson unconscious in the yard here. He's in one of those ambulances and… we already have Pierce in custody. They just stopped him at a roadblock."

"That's great news on both accounts." Austin nudged his chin behind them. "Walter Benally's back there at the bottom of a cliff. I'll give you directions."

"We'll take care of him." McGuire nodded to another officer and the man turned away to follow McGuire's unspoken order.

An ambulance driver tried to help Susan out of the speeder but she grasped Dulcie's hand as she passed. "I'm not going without you."

Dulcie sent a questioning glance at Austin.

He nodded. "It's okay. Go with her. Those cuts on your wrist need attention."

"I'm not going without you either."

McGuire stepped forward. "That's no problem. He's going to the hospital too. He looks like he took a pretty solid beating."

Austin grinned and grasped Dulcie's hand. "That's fine with me. I won't be letting this woman out of my sight for a long time to come." He paused and looked deep into her eyes. "Maybe ever."

Dulcie cupped the uninjured side of his face and pulled him down for another kiss.

* * * * *

Hello Dear Reader,

With this book, *Vanished in the Mountains*, I was able to return to one of my favorite places. I was born in southern Colorado but we moved when I was young. Many years later my husband and I returned. I was surprised by how much it felt like home to me. We camped on the edge of the Canyon de Chelly in a Navajo-owned campground without electricity or running water. Sitting in our motor home amid the piñon pines, we looked out over a valley with a view that stretched for hundreds of miles. A flat-topped mesa stood guard in the distance. As the sun set, the sky turned from pink to mauve and then purple. Watching, I finally understood why so many Native American paintings contain those colors. They arise from the natural elements of this wonderful land. We also watched storm clouds cross the sky and soon, lightning bolts reaching from the heavens to the ground, flashed across the dark horizon. It was an amazing experience. Canyon de Chelly will forever live in my memory. In this story, I hope I've captured some of the wonder of that unique place for you.

Blessings,
Tanya Stowe
www.tanyastowe.com

When search-and-rescue park ranger Autumn Mercer and her K-9 partner, Sherlock, meet a stranger in the mountains whose brother has gone missing, they drop everything to join the search. But with a storm and gunmen closing in, can she and Derek Peterson survive long enough to complete their mission?

Read on for a sneak preview of
Mountain Survival *by Christy Barritt,*
available March 2021 from Love Inspired Suspense.

After another bullet whizzed by, Autumn turned, trying to get a better view of the gunman. She had to figure out where he was.

"Stay behind the tree," she whispered to Derek. "And keep an eye on Sherlock."

Finally, she spotted a gunman crouched behind a nearby boulder. The front of his Glock was pointed at her.

A Glock? The man definitely wasn't a hunter.

Autumn already knew that, though.

Hunters didn't aim their guns at people.

Her gaze continued to scan the area. She spotted another man behind a tree and a third man behind another boulder.

Who were these guys? And what did they want from Autumn?

Backup couldn't get here soon enough.

The breeze picked up again, bringing another smattering of rain with it. They didn't have much time here. The conditions were going to become perilous at any minute. The storm might drive the gunman away, but it would present other dangers in the process.

She spotted a fourth man behind another tree in the distance. They all surrounded the campsite where Derek and his brother had set up.

They'd been waiting for Derek to return, hadn't they?

Why? What sense did that make?

She didn't have time to think about that now. Another bullet came flying past, piercing a nearby tree.

"What are we going to do?" Derek whispered. "Can I help?"

"Just stay behind a tree and remain quiet," she said. "We don't want to make this too easy for them."

Sherlock let out a little whine, but Autumn shushed the dog.

The man fired again. This time the bullet split the wood only inches from her.

Autumn's heart raced. These men were out for blood.

Even if the men ran out of bullets, she and Derek were going to be outnumbered. They couldn't just wait here for that to happen.

She had to act—and now.

She turned, pulling her gun's trigger.

Don't miss
Mountain Survival *by Christy Barritt,*
available March 2021 wherever Love Inspired Suspense
books and ebooks are sold.

LoveInspired.com

LISEXP0221